GHOSTLY INTERESTS
A HARPER HARLOW MYSTERY BOOK ONE

LILY HARPER HART

HARPERHART PUBLICATIONS

Copyright © 2015 by Lily Harper Hart

All rights reserved.

No part of this book may be reproduced in any form or by any electronic or mechanical means, including information storage and retrieval systems, without written permission from the author, except for the use of brief quotations in a book review.

❦ Created with Vellum

PROLOGUE

TWENTY YEARS AGO

Harper Harlow woke up to an odd feeling.

She was in her bed, turned on her side in the same position as when she fell asleep hours before, but something was different.

Harper was braver than most eight-year-olds and yet the sense of panic settling in her chest was something she couldn't explain or control. She wasn't alone. She could feel it.

She opened her mouth, a scream on her lips, but then she heard a familiar voice in the darkness.

"It's just me, kiddo."

"Gramps?" Harper's voice was thick with sleep. "I ... what are you doing here? Is something wrong?" Harper rubbed her eyes, trying to clear them so she could see through the murky darkness. When she finally caught sight of the figure standing next to the bed he brought more questions to her mind than answers. "You look funny."

Earl Harlow graced his favorite grandchild with a sad smile. "I feel funny," he said. "I ... just wanted to see you before I go."

"Where are you going?"

"Away," Earl said. "I'll be away for a long time. I didn't want to leave without saying goodbye, though. I knew you wouldn't like that."

"Did you say goodbye to Mom and Dad?" Harper was having

trouble understanding what was happening. Her grandfather lived in the same small town she did, so he often stopped by to see her. He took her to the New Baltimore pier so they could fish and eat hot dogs. He took her to the Detroit Zoo because she loved the animals. He took her to the Henry Ford Museum because he loved history and wanted to pass that love along to her. In all his visits, though, Harper could never remember him showing up in her bedroom in the middle of the night.

"I said goodbye to your parents," Earl said, choosing his words carefully. "They might not realize it, but I did."

"I ... how come you're here?" Harper asked, her mind still muddled.

"Because you're the one who is going to miss me the most," Earl said. "I have faith that you'll ... understand ... why I had to go one day."

"Where are you going?"

"To a ... new ... place," Earl said.

"A better place?"

"No place can be better without you there," Earl said. "It's a happy place, though."

"Is Grammy going with you?" Harper asked, confused. "Why didn't she come to say goodbye?"

"Grammy is staying behind," Earl said. "She's going to be sad for a little while so I need you to spend time with her – even if you don't want to. Take her to the pier. She'll put up a fight at first, but she'll enjoy it eventually. When you go there I want you to talk about me."

"But you won't be there?" Harper's lower lip trembled. "Why not?"

"I can't go there with you," Earl explained. "I have to leave." He tilted his head to the side as a phone rang in the bowels of the house. "I can't be here much longer," he said. "I'm almost out of time. I wanted to tell you how much I love you before I go, though. I've loved you since the moment your father introduced us."

"I love you, too," Harper said, pushing her flyaway blond hair away from her face. She slept hard and her hair reflected that every morning. "When will I see you again?"

"Not for a long time, kiddo," Earl said. "I'll always be watching you, though. Sometimes you'll think you see something out of the corner of your eye. That will be me. I'll always be watching you and I'll always love you. Never forget that."

"But...."

Earl shook his head. "Your mom is coming now. She has something bad to tell you. It's okay. I'm okay. I'll see you again. I promise."

"I don't understand," Harper whispered. "I ... why do you have to go?"

"It's my time," Earl said, shifting his attention to Harper's bedroom door as it opened.

Gloria Harlow, her eyes red-rimmed and glassy, moved into her daughter's bedroom. "Harlow, what are you doing up?"

"I...."

Gloria shook her head, her own blond hair mussed from sleep as she jerked her chin back and forth. "It doesn't matter," she said. "Sweetheart, I have some bad news."

Harper glanced at her grandfather. He was watching the scene from the corner and she could almost swear he was disappearing in front of her very eyes. What was going on here? "Mommy?"

"We lost your grandfather tonight, Harper," Gloria said, her voice soft.

"What do you mean?" Harper was on the verge of tears, warring thoughts colliding in a manner that caused mental clanging in the back of her mind.

"Grandpa passed away," Gloria said. "That was your grandmother on the phone. He had a heart attack in his sleep. He didn't feel any pain."

Harper's blue eyes darted to the corner. Earl was almost completely gone now. "He's here, though," Harper said. "I ... he came to see me."

"I'm sure he'll always be watching you, Harper," Gloria said, reaching for her daughter to soothe her with a hug. "He loved you so much."

"But he's here," Harper argued. "I ... ." She turned her head so she could stare into the corner again. It was empty. "He was here. I saw him. I talked to him."

"He's been gone for hours, Harper," Gloria said. "I think you had a dream. It's nice you dreamed about him on the same night we ... lost ... him." Gloria choked up and struggled to refrain from body-wracking sobs in an effort to protect her daughter. "You'll always have good memories."

Harper couldn't wrap her head around what was going on. "But he was here," she said. "He said he had to go away but I would see him again. He said ... he was right here."

"Shh, Harper," Gloria said, smoothing her daughter's hair down as she rocked her. "It's okay. Everything is going to be okay."

Was it? Harper wasn't so sure. The only thing she could be sure about was that nothing was ever going to be the same again. She didn't know how she knew that ... but she did.

ONE

PRESENT DAY

"Look out behind you!"

Zander Pritchett was beside himself as he watched his best friend duck behind an ornamental column, sliding on the glazed hardwood dance floor as she careened out of the way of something he couldn't see and yet still knew was there. A glass vase shattered against the floor in the exact spot she was standing only seconds before.

They were at Undercurrents, a fancy waterfront restaurant on Lake St. Clair on Harsens Island in Southeastern Michigan, and their current job was turning into a righteous fright fest.

"What do you see?" Harper asked, her shoulder-length blond hair standing out at odd angles as she surveyed the room.

"You know very well I don't see ghosts," Zander said, his hands on his narrow hips as he regarded Harlow from across the room. "I don't think now is the time for jokes."

"I wasn't making a joke," Harper snapped, rolling her eyes despite the circumstances. "I wasn't even talking to you. I was talking to Molly."

"Oh," Zander said. "I ... you don't have to be so snippy."

"A ghost is trying to flatten me, Zander," Harper shot back. "I think now is the time to be snippy."

"Whatever," Zander said, pressing his back to the wall and lifting the walkie-talkie to his face. "Molly, what do you see on the thermal scanner?"

From the manager's office where she was set up, twenty-one-year-old Molly Parker enthusiastically regaled Zander with a litany of mumbo jumbo that essentially meant she had no idea what she was looking at. She was extremely enthusiastic about it, though.

"Be specific," Zander ordered. "Is there more than one ghost in here or not?"

"I'm only seeing one cold spot," Molly said primly, and although Zander couldn't see her pert features he could imagine the face she was probably making. "It's right by Harper."

Don West, the owner of Undercurrents, hired Ghost Hunters, Inc. – GHI for those in the inner circle – the day before because he couldn't handle one more interrupted wedding or tearful bride complaining that a pesky poltergeist ruined the biggest day of her life. He didn't believe in the paranormal, but he saw no way out of his predicament other than hiring Macomb County's leading ghost hunters. From his spot next to Zander, he was less than impressed. "There's nothing there," he said. "Your friend is ducking like something is there, but so far all we've seen is a glass vase hurtling across the room – and I haven't ruled you guys out as somehow causing that."

Zander shot West a hard look. "You hired us, remember?"

"I remember," West said. "You also promised you would handle my … little problem … with the utmost delicacy. This doesn't look delicate to me."

Zander pushed his floppy brown hair off of his forehead as he wiped the accumulating sweat away from his angular face. "We can't do anything until we identify what kind of spirit you have here."

West narrowed his eyes. "Are you sure this isn't a scam?"

As if on cue another vase lifted from a nearby table and flew through the air, not stopping until it smashed into the wall about a foot from West's head.

"Do you think we faked that?" Zander asked pointedly.

"I ... ." West broke off, worrying his bottom lip with his teeth. "You have to do something about this. We're going to lose money if it gets out that we're the place for haunted weddings. We're coming up on our busiest six months of the year."

"To be fair, some people would love a haunted wedding," Zander replied, ducking as another vase smashed into the wall. "This might be a little extreme for most people, though," he conceded. "I ... ."

"As much as I'm enjoying this conversation, can you focus on me?" Harper interrupted, her blue eyes flashing impatiently. "I'm the one exposed here."

"You're such a pill sometimes," Zander grumbled. "What do you want me to do? You know darned well I can't see anything. I'm supposed to be your emotional support and tech guy. I don't do well with the hands-on stuff."

"I need you to set the trap," Harper said, making a face. "Throw it out in the middle of the room. I'll take care of leading the ghost there."

"How?" Zander furrowed his brow. "Are you going to run out into the open and lead the ghost over the trap?"

"Yes."

"But ... what if it catches you?" Zander asked, hoping he didn't sound as terrified as he felt. He made a living catching ghosts with his lifelong best friend, but he was less than thrilled with the means they utilized to do it. "What if it ... hurts ... you?"

"I'll be fine, Zander," Harper said, meeting his gaze evenly from across the room. "I'm right here. The spirit is attracted to me. It's going to be watching me. That's going to give you the opportunity to set the trap."

"What if it decides I'm better looking?" Zander asked, buying time as he tried to tug on his hidden courage. "You said the spirit's energy felt female. She's going to find me more attractive than you."

"You're gay." Harper was nonplussed as she straightened and wiped her sweaty palms against her pants.

"She doesn't know that," Zander replied. "All she knows is that I'm hotter than anyone she's ever seen before and she'd like to take a ghostly bite out of my shapely butt. She doesn't know or care that I'm gay."

"I see you've given this a lot of thought," Harper deadpanned, smirking. "Whoever this woman is she's been haunting this location for years. I don't think she's worried about your rear end – no matter how shapely it is."

"Maybe she died of a broken heart because the man she was in love with looked like me," Zander suggested. "She could totally fixate on me because I could be the reincarnated soul of her dead lover."

"You really have to start watching something else besides Lifetime," Harper said, her aggravation growing with each passing second. "Now get the trap and get moving. I don't want to spend all day here and Mr. West mentioned something about a lunch serving that starts in an hour. We have to do this, and we have to do it now."

"And you have to do it with minimal property damage and as quietly as possible," West chimed in. "Don't break anything."

"We'll do our best," Zander said, clicking his heels together and mock saluting before he leaned over and started rummaging through the duffel bag at his feet. A few moments later he straightened again.

West eyed the contraption in his hand dubiously. "What is that?"

"It's a ghost snare."

"But … it looks like one of those things you can buy at the flea market … what do they call them … dreamcatchers," West said. "It looks like a dreamcatcher."

"It is," Zander said, gritting his teeth to keep from snapping at the man who would be handing over a paycheck in about ten minutes. "It's infused with holy water, salt and rosemary."

"And that catches ghosts?" West looked dubious.

"Kind of," Zander hedged. "One other thing needs to happen, too."

"What?"

"Watch," Zander said. He exchanged one more look with Harper. "Here I go."

Harper smiled at him, the expression not quite making it to her eyes but still heartfelt. "Good luck."

"You, too." Zander clutched the dreamcatcher in his hand and then sprinted into the middle of the room, surprising West with his speed and agility. Zander dropped the dreamcatcher on the dance floor and continued running until he was on the other side of the room. He was still separated from Harper, but he was a lot nearer than he was only seconds before.

Harper lifted her walkie-talkie to her ear. "Eric, are you ready with the EMF to take measurements for us to study later?"

From his spot at the far end of the room, Eric Tyler shot Harper a thumbs-up. Even though it was hot in the room he was still wearing a leather jacket and his long, black hair brushed the top of his shoulders as he hopped from one foot to the other in anticipation.

"Okay," Harper said, sucking in a breath. "Here we go."

"Harper ... be careful," Zander warned.

"I'm always careful."

That was kind of the truth and kind of a lie at the same time, but Zander let it slide as he watched his best friend in the world gear up for her big run. "I'm right here," he said. "I'll be close."

"You always are," Harper said, grinning as she collected her courage.

When Harper raced to the center of the room it looked as if she was going to overshoot her mark. The haunting howling chased her and the ethereal spirit seemed surprised when it realized Harper was not only stopping but also turning back.

Harper placed one foot on the dreamcatcher and faced off with the ghost. "I release you to the other side," she said, clapping her hands together and causing a "spark" to flood the room.

West sheltered his eyes with his forearm while Zander tried to watch the scene in its entirety and failed.

The light swallowed up Harper as an angry ghost descended upon her.

It was time.

. . .

"**I DON'T** know what to say," West said, eyeing Harper as she handed the dreamcatcher to Zander a few minutes later. "I ... where did the light come from?"

Harper wasn't one to discuss her abilities – or how they worked. That could have something to do with the fact that she had no idea how she managed to do the fantastical things she did – and it could also have a little something to do with the fact that people didn't believe her no matter what she told them.

"That was the trap being activated," Harper explained. "There's a bright light associated with the gate opening. It sucks the ghost in." That wasn't technically a lie. It wasn't technically the truth either.

"But ... how?" West pressed.

"It's an old tactic handed down through the centuries," Harper said. "We read about it in a book, tried it, and it worked." Zander glanced at Harper, a silent warning on his pursed lips. Harper ignored him. "It's folk magic."

West made a face? "Magic? I don't believe in magic."

"You said you don't believe in ghosts either and you just watched us catch one," Harper pointed out.

"I'm not sure what I saw," West said. "How do I know what really happened? You guys have a lot of equipment. It could've been a fancy light show and nothing more."

"I guess it's your prerogative to believe that," Harper said, forcing her face to remain neutral. She was used to people calling her theatrical. That was actually one of the nicer terms bandied in her direction. It was when they called her a liar that she started taking offense.

"How much do I owe you?" West asked.

"A thousand dollars," Zander said. "We settled on a price over the phone. That's why we agreed to come out here in the first place." He was feigning patience, but Harper could see his hackles rising.

"That's way too much for a glorified light show," West argued. "How do I know the problem won't return the second you leave?"

"Sir, we agreed upon a price ... ." Zander didn't get a chance to finish his sentence because Harper was reaching for the dreamcatcher.

"If you don't want to pay us we'll release the ghost and call it a day," she said. "I'm too tired to put up with this crap. We agreed on a price and now you're trying to go back on your word. I can't stand that."

"You can't simply return it," West said. "I ... that's unethical."

"We held up our end of the bargain," Harper reminded him. "You didn't. Who is unethical in that scenario?"

"But ... ."

"Sir, it doesn't matter if Harper releases the spirit or not," Zander said. "You signed an electronic agreement when I sent you the itemized estimate. You're legally bound to pay your bill.

"If you don't pay your bill then Harper is going to release the spirit," he continued. "You can cancel all of your summer weddings because it's really going to be ticked off now. Then we'll let this wind through the court system and, since we have your electronic signature, you're going to have to pay anyway."

West's cheeks reddened. "You can't possibly think ... ."

"Release the spirit," Zander said, his eyes never moving from West's murderous face as he talked to Harper.

"You've got it," Harper said, smiling sunnily in West's direction. "Good luck with catching this thing again. It's not going to fall for that gag twice."

"Wait!" West was defeated. Zander knew it. Harper knew it. The only one having trouble swallowing it was the man in charge. "Don't release it. I'll cut you a check right now."

"We agreed on cash," Zander said, his face immovable.

West scowled. "Fine. I'll get your cash. Just ... take that thing out of here."

"As soon as we have our money we will," Zander said.

Once West was out of earshot so he could gather the funds Zander shot Harper an appraising look. "You used the whole *Ghostbusters* hotel scene to snooker him," he said. "He honestly thought there was something there to release back into his restaurant."

"I'm starting to think we should collect the money upfront," Harper said.

"I'm starting to think you're right," Zander said. "Still ... that was inspired."

"I have my moments," Harper drawled. "They're many and varied."

"You're humble, too," Zander teased.

"Let's get our money and get out of here," Harper said. "I'm starving. Sending tortured souls to the hereafter really works up an appetite."

TWO

Jared Monroe ran his hand over his stubbled chin and gazed down at the ravaged body at his feet. He had no idea how his first case with the Whisper Cove Police Department turned out to be a murder, but that was exactly what he was looking at.

"What do we have?" Jared's new partner, Mel Kelsey, was in his early fifties and he looked just as flummoxed by the nude body on the beach as Jared felt. "Do we have an identity yet?"

"There was no clothing so there's no identification," Jared replied, his eyes weary as he scanned the long auburn hair splayed out on the beach. "We're going to need to run fingerprints and get this body moved to the medical examiner's facility down in Mount Clemens for a proper autopsy. When is the coroner's van supposed to get here?"

"Soon," Mel said. "They don't have to come up here very often so I had to give the secretary on the phone directions. She didn't even know there was a town north of New Baltimore on Lake St. Clair."

Whisper Cove was a small community hugging the border of St. Clair and Macomb counties in Southeastern Michigan. When Jared left the west side of the state to come east he initially envisioned landing in a crime-laden community closer to Detroit. He yearned for high stakes crimes and intricate investigations. Shrinking state budgets forced most of the suburban police departments to cut back instead of bolster dwindling law enforcement ranks, though, and Jared wasn't about to take on a beat in Detroit if he could help it. He wanted excitement, but he wasn't sure if he could take that much of it.

"Have you gathered any evidence?" Mel asked.

"I've really only done a cursory inspection," Jared said. "Have the techs finished taking photographs?"

Mel nodded.

"I guess now is as good of a time as any to start gathering evidence," Jared said, sighing heavily as he hunkered down next to the woman on the ground. "We have what looks to be a young woman in her early twenties. Her fingernails are well maintained, although the index fingernail is ripped off and ragged. It might mean she struggled with her assailant. We should make sure the medical examiner takes clippings."

"Don't they always do that?"

Jared had no idea. He wasn't familiar with how things worked in Macomb County yet. This was his second day on the job. When he took the position in Whisper Cove he figured it would get him in the right area to move on to a bigger department down the line. He never imagined murder would be on the menu ... especially this quickly. "They probably do," he conceded. "I want to make sure we cover all our bases, though. A lot of people are going to be looking at us."

"You've got that right," Mel said. "This is the first murder in Whisper Cove in ... well ... I've been here thirty years and the only one I can think of is Stan Sully."

"Who was he?"

"He was a local farmer who fell on his thresher."

"I thought you said it was a murder?" Jared pressed, confused.

"We found out he had help when he fell," Mel explained. "His wife Sally found out he was sleeping with the barmaid down at Whisper Winery and she didn't take it well."

"You had a woman named Sally Sully?" Jared wanted to laugh, but the dead body gave him pause. "I guess she was bound to crack eventually."

"Probably," Mel said, shrugging. "This one looks pretty... beat up."

"She does," Jared agreed, shifting his body so he could study the woman's long legs. "She's got a lot of bruises. It looks like she might've been tossed around a bit before she was killed."

"What do you think the cause of death is?" Mel asked. "She's got a lot of smaller wounds, and some of them are open, but there's no big wound that would signify how she died."

"I'm guessing she was either strangled or drowned," Jared replied. "The medical examiner will have to make that determination. I would have to guess that foul play is involved, though. She's naked, after all."

"Not necessarily," Mel hedged. "She could've been skinny-dipping and lost her bearings. The bruises could be from banging against rocks. It might be an accidental drowning."

"Isn't it a bit early in the season to be swimming in the lake?" Jared asked. "That water can't be much more than fifty degrees. It's still early in the season."

Spring in Michigan is usually short. Winter hangs on longer than people would like and spring lasts for about five weeks before summer descends. Jared knew the waters were too cold to swim in recreationally. He figured his partner was grasping at straws because he didn't want to believe there was a killer on the loose in the tiny hamlet.

"Maybe she was drunk," Mel suggested. "I know I've thought plenty of stupid things were good ideas when I had liquid courage to bolster me."

It was a possibility, but Jared wasn't banking on it. "We need to see what the medical examiner says before we make any decisions," he said. "We need an identification. Do you recognize her?"

"No," Mel said, shaking his head. "She's not from Whisper Cove. I think I know practically everyone here."

"That means she's probably from one of the surrounding communities," Jared mused. "Until we know how she died – and who she is – all we have are questions."

Mel lifted his head and inclined his chin to the parking lot of the nearby restaurant. "I think we're about to get some of those answered," he said. "The medical examiner is here."

"DO YOU want me to burn this?" Molly lifted the dreamcatcher up, wrinkling her nose at the scent. "It smells like someone died."

"Technically they did," Harper said. "Yeah, go ahead and burn it."

Dreamcatcher traps were only good for one use and after the soul was displaced from one plane of existence to the next it was customary to burn them to make sure no negative residue remained.

Harper watched the energetic college student walk out through the back door of the office, internally marveling at her blond hair – which was often streaked with some vibrant shade of Manic Panic – and couldn't help but smile. She admired Molly's enthusiasm and insistence on being who she wanted to be. The pink streaks in her hair this week were a little more garish than Harper would be comfortable sporting, but the St. Clair Community College student somehow made them work.

"I can't believe you let her come to work with her hair like that," Eric grumbled. He was busy uploading the data from the EMF recorder to his computer and he didn't look happy. At twenty-five, he was a few years younger than Harper and Zander but a few years older than Molly. He was in a tough spot in the office, mostly because he had a huge crush on Harper that she pretended not to notice and Molly had a huge crush on him that he opted to ignore. It was a vicious – and often soap opera resembling – circle.

"I like her hair," Harper said. "She's young. When you're twenty-one you should have odd hair. That's when you can pull it off without judgment."

"She's representing your company, though," Eric reminded her. "Doesn't it bug you that people see a ... hippie ... when they look at her?"

Harper shrugged. "Not really," she said. "People already look at me funny. I run a ghost hunting business," she said, chuckling harshly. "People are always going to think I'm crazy."

"I guess," Eric said. "She should still present herself in a professional manner."

"She's an unpaid intern," Harper reminded him. "She can dress how she wants. I can't make demands on her appearance if I'm not going to pay her. She's not technically an employee."

"Right," Eric said. "Why is she here again?"

"Because she wanted to learn the ropes and she has great computer skills," Harper replied, not missing a beat. "I don't understand why you can't be nicer to her."

"She's always ... staring at me," Eric said, his dark eyes serious. "It makes me uncomfortable. It's as if she's undressing me with her eyes."

Harper knew exactly how he felt. It was an emotion near and dear to her heart whenever Eric got that moony look on his face where she was concerned. She enjoyed the local tech guru's company – and even found him attractive – but there was no sexual chemistry there. Eric didn't appear to recognize that, though.

"She has a crush on you," Harper said. "You should be flattered. In ten years, you're going to wish a twenty-one-year-old with a body like that had a crush on you."

"Her body isn't that great," Eric argued.

Harper arched an eyebrow. "I would kill for her body."

"Your body is so much better," Eric said. "I'll bet you look great without your clothes on."

Harper's cheeks burned under Eric's earnest expression. The man fancied himself "bad to the bone," even riding a motorcycle to cement his perceived reputation. The problem for Eric was that he was much more Fonzie on *Happy Days* than Jax on *Sons of Anarchy*. He just didn't seem to realize it. "I ... um ... thank you," Harper said, hoping to steer the conversation back to a safer topic. "Did you get anything from the capture at Undercurrents?"

"It's going to take some time to go through the data," Eric said. "It's too soon to tell what we're looking at. I got some good thermal video, though. I'm not sure what we have yet."

"Well, don't worry about rushing," Harper said. "We don't have another client today so you can spend the rest of the afternoon going over your data. I know how you love those little chart things you do."

Eric scowled. "Chart things? I'll have you know ... ."

"That those are vital statistical analysis tools that will propel our knowledge of the hereafter into uncharted territory," Zander said, breezing into the room as he mimicked Eric's voice. "We know. You've told us a zillion times."

"Then how come you keep forgetting?"

"My memory isn't what it used to be," Zander deadpanned. "It was probably all that pot I smoked in high school."

"I'm so underappreciated," Eric muttered.

"I appreciate you," Harper said, shooting a dirty look in Zander's direction. "Can you please not poke the bear? He's going through some files for us and we should respect him because neither one of us wants to go through all of that information."

"Data," Eric corrected.

"Data," Harper said, pursing her lips as she tried to ignore Zander's vigorous eye rolling. "It's very important data and Eric deserves your respect."

"Whatever," Zander said, sighing with resigned exasperation. "I don't suppose you would give me the respect I so richly deserve and take me to the lunch you promised, would you?"

"It's still early," Harper protested.

"My stomach doesn't agree," Zander said, lifting his shirt and pointing toward his eight-pack abs. "My stomach says it's feeding time."

Harper snorted. "You lifted your shirt because you like to show off your abs. Admit it."

"I'll admit nothing of the sort."

"If you don't admit it I can't buy you lunch," Harper said.

Zander exhaled heavily, one of those extended gusts that only long-suffering best friends can get away with. "When you work out as much as I do, you should be able to show your body off without people commenting."

"I thought you wanted people to comment?" Harper pressed.

"You don't have the right parts to comment," Zander corrected. "Even if you did, though, you're like a sibling to me. I don't care how hot of a guy you would make, I'm not into the incest thing."

"This conversation is taking a gross turn," Eric said.

"He's right," Harper said. "Fine. I'll buy you lunch on one condition …."

"That I lift my shirt and wow the male waiter so we can get free dessert?" Zander asked.

"No," Harper said, her tone dry. "That you never bring up incest again. It makes me feel … uncomfortable."

"Fine," Zander conceded. "Can I still lift my shirt to wow the waiter?"

"Go nuts."

THREE

"This place has the best clam chowder in the world," Zander said, dipping his spoon into the thick white soup as he brandished a warm roll in Harper's face. "Why aren't you eating your lunch?"

Harper was lost in thought, her mind on the afternoon's ghost hunt instead of Zander's wild food proclamations. Ever since she was seven years old and her grandfather visited her after his death, the willowy blonde knew she was different. She screamed to the high heavens that her grandfather visited her that night – but no one believed her. They thought she was a sad little girl making up stories.

When she was in middle school and the lunch lady's ghost told her that her body was behind the Dumpster in the parking lot, everyone said Harper made a lucky guess but thanked her for helping put Darlene to rest before her body was covered with snow and possibly lost until spring.

When she was in high school and Tori Owens came to her after drinking too much beer at a keg party and Harper led police – and Tori's distraught parents – to the spot where panicked classmates dumped the teenager's body so they wouldn't get into trouble people started to look at her in a different way ... and it wasn't a friendly one.

It wasn't until her senior year that Whisper Cove lived up to its gossipy name, though. That was when a St. Clair County woman's ghost begged Harper for help and led her to the site of a car wreck – where her three-year-old daughter was still alive – that people started to realize that Harper Harlow was not a normal girl. She was ... special.

The big cable channels aired the story – and begged for interviews – but Harper declined every request. She wasn't looking for accolades. No, what she wanted was answers. They never came.

She had no idea how she sent spirits on their merry way. She simply knew that's what happened when she stomped her foot on the dreamcatcher and the bright light engulfed her. In that split second of illumination, she was caught between two worlds and she could see hints of movement from beyond before returning to Earth. She never saw faces, but she did immerse herself in the warm feelings. The money was nice, but it was the emotion of the other place that helped fuel her.

"Harper, what are you thinking about?" Zander asked, exasperated.

Harper forced her attention to her best friend. "I ... um ... what were we talking about?"

"I was going on and on about how great the soup was – and how hot the waiter is – and you were lost in another world," Zander said. "That's it, isn't it? You were thinking about that other world you see whenever you release a ghost, weren't you?"

"I can't help it," Harper admitted. "It's always such a ... great ... feeling. It takes me a few hours to come down. You know that."

Zander smiled fondly at her. "I do know that. Still ... we're here to talk about me. Do you think I should ask the waiter out?"

Harper glanced over her shoulder, studying the waiter in question for a moment. Donahue's Pub was Zander's current favorite place to eat thanks to the recent staff addition. He was young, buff, and openly flirtatious whenever Zander and Harlow visited. As much as she liked the soup, Harper was starting to yearn for more variety when it came to their lunchtime food choices.

"I think you should definitely ask him out," Harper said. "That way you can go on two dates and then break up with him for whatever nonsensical reason you come up with this time and we can go back to a few of the other restaurants in town."

"I do not have nonsensical reasons for dumping people," Zander argued. "My reasons are always sound."

"You broke up with the guy from the garage because he smelled like gasoline," Harper said. "What was his name again? Chet, right? You should've known he would smell like gasoline because he worked in a garage. That relationship was doomed from the start. Who names their kid Chet?"

"That was a family name," Zander said. "I didn't realize the smell of gasoline gave me a headache until it was too late. That was completely out of my control."

"What about the guy you met at the gym?" Harper asked.

"Don't bring him up."

Harper ignored Zander's admonishment. "You cruised him for a week straight," she said. "You even joined a water aerobics class because he was in it. You worked overtime to get him and what happened then?"

"He shaved his armpits," Zander argued. "I like a muscular guy and I like that whole metrosexual thing. I like a little manscaping. I don't trust anyone who shaves their armpits, though. That's just … wrong."

Harper pursed her lips to keep from laughing out loud. This was a fun game. "How about the guy you picked up at the deli?"

"Oh, I knew you were going to go there," Zander muttered.

"You were in love with him from afar because he always picked fresh produce and you were on a health kick," Harper said. "Why did that relationship last for exactly three dates again? Oh, that's right, you can't trust anyone who is vegan because if a person dislikes cheese that's the same thing as disliking America."

"I'm a patriot at heart," Zander sniffed.

Harper loved her best friend beyond reason, but his fickle nature irked her on the best of days. Two straight weeks of eating the same lunch on the same patio was getting old. She wanted Zander to ask the waiter out so he could dump him before the following week. She wasn't having clam chowder for lunch again – not until the fall when soup was a welcome meal.

"Ask him out," Harper prodded. "We both know you want to. Heck, he knows you want to. If you do it now we can go back to that place that has that great Creole shrimp dish next week. I've been dreaming about that."

"You need to find a man so you can dream about something spicier than food," Zander said, making a face. "Seriously, why don't you go out with Eric? He loves you. He worships the ground you walk on."

"There's no sexual chemistry there," Harper replied. "I'm not attracted to him. He's a nice guy. He's too young for me, though."

"He's three years younger than you," Zander countered. "It's not like you're Mrs. Robinson ... or that creepy teacher who got knocked up by her student twice and then ended up marrying him."

"Thanks for *that* visual," Harper said, shaking her head. "I'm not really in a place where a relationship makes sense right now. You know that."

"I think you're scared to be in a relationship because you're only attracted to non-believers and they all think you're strange when you admit you can see and talk to ghosts."

"I ... you're a pain," Harper muttered.

"And yet you love me anyway," Zander said. "Eat your soup. Once you're done I'll hit on the waiter and we can get going. I'm ready to blow this popsicle stand. Yes, I heard the double entendre the second I said it. There's no reason to comment on it."

HARPER BUSIED herself on the beach while Zander prettied himself up in the bathroom, visions of getting busy with the waiter practically lifting like thought bubbles from his head.

Spring in Michigan was one of her favorite times of the year. The trees were budding, the grass was greening, and the air smelled of possibilities. Zander often fell under the spring's thrall when it came to his dating life. That wasn't a surprise. He liked the idea of falling in love more than the reality of having to put up with someone else's quirks. Since Zander and Harper shared a house, Harper was often relieved Zander was incapable of settling down. While she knew they couldn't live together forever, the idea of separating from her strongest ally was troubling.

It wasn't something she was going to have to worry about today – or tomorrow even. It was inevitable, though. Sooner or later one or both of them was going to find someone to settle down with. Given Harper's lack of a dating life, odds were that Zander was the one who was destined to be hit by the love truck first.

Harper was so lost in thought she didn't notice she wasn't alone until she caught a hint of movement out of the corner of her eye. She snapped her head up, an apology on her lips in case she was blocking someone from their path to the water, but the words died on her lips when she saw the ghost.

"Hi," Harper said, sighing loudly when she saw the auburn-haired woman. She was dressed in simple jeans and a T-shirt, and her peaches-and-cream complexion glowed with the appearance of life even as her ethereal body was proof of death. "What are you doing here?"

The ghost widened her eyes in surprise. Harper had no idea how long she'd been wandering aimlessly, but it was clear she didn't think anyone could see her.

"You're dead," Harper said, nodding sadly. "I ... do you know how you died?"

The woman opened her mouth as if to respond and then snapped it shut, her ghostly hand flying to her lips as she absorbed Harper's words.

"It's okay," Harper said softly. "I want to help you. If you tell me what happened I might be able to help you move on."

The ghost remained rooted to her spot, immovable and silent as she tried to come to terms with her new reality. Harper realized the woman might be laboring under the delusion this wasn't really happening to her – or she was dreaming. That meant her death was fresh ... and possibly violent.

"Who are you talking to?" Zander asked, bounding to Harper's side as he slipped a folded sheet of paper into his pocket. "Mission accomplished, by the way. I got his number and a promise of a good time."

"There's a ghost here," Harper said, ignoring Zander's side jaunt to La-La Land. "I think she's new."

"So send her on her way," Zander suggested. "Do you want to get some ice cream? I know it's early in the season, but ice cream sounds good. I'll have to work it off at the gym later, but something tells me I'm up for the challenge."

Harper kept her eyes fixed on the distraught woman. "I think she's really new," she said. "Like ... a few hours new."

"That's horrible," Zander said, his compassion on spring break. "Send her to your favorite hereafter and let's go."

"She's young, Zander."

"So? She probably died in an accident or something." Harper's earnest nature and determination to help the dead proved both lucrative and annoying to Zander on a daily basis. He loved her, but he often wanted to shake her. "Where did we come down on the ice cream decision?"

The ghost's gaze bounced between Zander and Harper a moment, her face boasting a myriad of emotions that ranged from anger, hurt, and worry to hope, relief, and calm. Then, without saying a word, she turned on her filmy heel and moved away from Harper, fixing her course in the direction of the water line.

"We have to follow her," Harper said. "I think that's what she wants us to do."

"What about the ice cream?"

"I'll buy a pint of Ben & Jerry's on my way home tonight," Harper said, wrapping her fingers around Zander's wrist and tugging him behind her. "Come on."

"But ... ."

"Come on!"

Zander knew better than to argue with her when she got in one of her moods. Twenty-three years together had taught him she couldn't be talked down from a virtual ledge. She always had to jump.

Zander and Harper were almost to the pier when the swirling

police lights finally registered. Harper lifted her eyes to scan the beach, and when she shifted her attention back to Zander they both knew what they were dealing with.

"Oh, crap," Zander complained. "They're here for her dead body, aren't they?"

"I think so," Harper said. "What are the odds someone else died here and she led us to another body?"

"How can this happen on my happy day?" Zander groused. "I'm not sure how, but I'm totally blaming you for this."

FOUR

"Who is that?" Jared asked, lifting his blue eyes from the industrious medical examiner and focusing on the couple standing at the edge of the crime scene.

Mel followed Jared's gaze, smirking when his eyes landed on Harper and Zander. "Oh, well, I shouldn't be surprised," he said. "Where there's death there's Harper Harlow."

"What does that mean?" Jared asked, confused.

Mel didn't answer. Instead he left his partner to oversee the medical examiner's final task – loading the body into a bag – and trudged toward the familiar faces. "Kids," Mel said, teasing the duo affectionately.

"What's going on, Uncle Mel?" Zander asked. "Did someone drown?"

"We don't know yet," Mel said. "A morning walker discovered a body on the beach. We're trying to ascertain how she died."

"She probably got drunk and decided to take a swim," Zander said.

"That's what I said." Mel grinned at his sister's son. "Great minds think alike, huh?"

"It must be in the genes," Zander agreed.

"Why are you two here?" Mel asked, shifting his gaze to Harlow. "Are you ghost busting?"

While Mel was one of Zander's favorite uncles he was also of the mind that Zander and Harlow were basically performing theater instead of working when they rid property of ghosts. Because he loved his uncle, Zander ignored the digs. Harper didn't have such an easy time with it.

"Who is the woman who died?"

"Who told you it was a woman?" Jared appeared behind Mel, his intense eyes landing on Harper.

"I . . . ." Harper wasn't sure how to answer.

"We guessed," Zander answered smoothly. "You must be Jared Monroe. I heard you were coming to town."

"And who are you?" Jared asked, his eyes bouncing from Harper to Zander and then back again. Her face was magnetic and he found he didn't want to look elsewhere.

"This is my nephew," Mel said quickly. "He's my sister's boy. Zander Pritchett, this is my new partner. Make sure you show him some respect."

"It's nice to meet you," Zander said, extending his hand.

"You, too," Jared said, his face softening even though his shoulders remained stiff. "You didn't answer how you knew the body belonged to a woman."

"We assumed it was a woman because the people up by the café told us a female body was found down here," Zander lied.

"How did they find out?" Jared was incensed.

"It's a small town," Mel said, rolling his eyes. "You're going to realize you can't bend over to get a pebble out of your shoe in Whisper Cove without everyone knowing it."

"I guess," Jared said, scowling as he met Harper's studied gaze. There was something about her face that appealed to him – and not in the obvious way. She was beautiful, her eyes sparkly, but there was something else about her he couldn't put his finger on. "And who are you?"

"I'm sorry," Mel said, rubbing his hands together sheepishly. "My manners are shot today. This is Harper Harlow. She's my nephew's ... "

"Girlfriend?" Jared supplied, hoping the answer would be yes so he could immediately tamp the physical attraction coursing through him down. He wasn't ready to contemplate dating any of Whisper Cove's finest – mostly because he had no intention of making the small town his permanent home. He didn't need any romantic entanglements.

Mel, Zander, and Harper burst into simultaneous guffaws.

"What did I say?" Jared asked, confused.

"Harper isn't my girlfriend," Zander explained. "We live together – but not in sin."

"I'm not sure I understand," Jared hedged.

"I'm gay," Zander said.

"You probably shouldn't announce that to strangers, boy," Mel admonished him. "They might not like it."

"You don't like it," Zander countered. "You still think it's a phase I'm going through. It's not. I was born this way. I like boys. You're going to have to deal with it."

"You're my favorite nephew and I have dealt with it," Mel said. "I just don't see why it's necessary for you to announce to anyone who will listen that you ... do that stuff."

Jared couldn't hide his smirk. "I'm fine with it," he said. "I think it's great Zander has no problem being himself. That shows he has character."

"That shows he *is* a character," Mel corrected. "The boy popped out of my sister's womb shouting to the high heavens. He hasn't stopped since."

"You're still mad I made you come to all three showings of the high school musical, aren't you?" Zander teased.

"No one needs to see *Grease* that many times," Mel grumbled.

"You got off easy," Harper said. "I had to do his makeup *and* watch the show. Talk about torture."

Mel snorted while Jared looked Harper up and down. She was thinly built, her waist narrow and her legs long. Her cheeks were high and angular, and the petulant pout of her lips looked naturally pink. She stood out in a town the size of Whisper Cove.

"And you two live together?" Jared asked, trying to get a handle on the relationship between Zander and Harper.

"We do," Zander said. "We decided to buy a house together two years ago. Pooling our money allowed us to buy this great place out by the lake. We don't have waterfront property, but we can walk there in five minutes."

"What happens if one of you ... hooks up?" Jared asked.

"We put a tie on our bedroom doors and promise not to listen," Zander deadpanned. "What do you think happens? We're roommates, not each other's keepers."

"I'm sorry," Jared said, holding his hands up. "I didn't mean anything. I've just never seen people as old as the two of you living together out of choice."

"What is that supposed to mean?" Harper asked, her hands moving to her hips. "There's nothing wrong with us living together."

"I didn't mean that the way it came out."

"Don't get your panties in a bunch, Harper," Mel warned. "Jared is new here and his first case is a naked woman on the beach who was probably murdered. We've both been thrown with this one."

"She was naked?" Harper asked, cocking an eyebrow.

"I probably shouldn't have said that," Mel said, rubbing the back of his neck.

"No," Jared agreed.

"Why was she naked?" Zander asked. "Was she ... ?" He didn't finish the sentence, the possibility too horrid to give it voice.

"We don't know anything yet so I don't want you two spreading rumors," Mel said. "In fact, you two shouldn't even be down here. You should be on your way."

"But ... ." Harper wanted to argue. She wanted to come up with a reason to stay. Her mind was a blank, though.

"Go," Mel prodded. "This has nothing to do with the two of you and your ... business."

"You don't know that," Zander shot back. "This very well could have something to do with our business."

"It doesn't." Mel's voice was firm. "Now ... off with the two of you."

"You're lucky I can't stay mad at you," Zander warned, grabbing Harper's elbow and starting to direct her away from the crime scene. "Come on. I think we're done here."

Harper's eyes met Jared's for one more moment, an invisible current passing between them, and then she reluctantly turned and followed her best friend. The dead woman stood next to her body, her eyes mournful as she watched the medical examiner tug the zipper up.

Harper silently offered a promise that she would return when the scene was cleared, although she knew the woman couldn't hear her.

"YOUR NEPHEW SEEMS NICE," Jared said, sliding a mug of coffee onto Mel's desk an hour later.

The two officers were in Whisper Cove's small police station, eager to work but hampered without the victim's identity to drum up leads. For now they were waiting for a call from the medical examiner. There was nothing else they could do but chat with one another until then. Since they were still getting to know one another, Jared took the opportunity to touch on Mel's family, figuring it was a safe subject. He was about to get an earful to the contrary.

"He's a good kid," Mel said. "He does weird things, but they're mostly from a good place and generally harmless."

"I'm not sure what that means."

"It's Harper," Mel explained. "Those two have been thicker than thieves since they sat next to each other in afternoon kindergarten twenty-three years ago."

"She seems nice enough," Jared said carefully. "I thought she was a little distracted, but other than that she was perfectly pleasant. Why don't you like her?"

"I love Harper," Mel said. "She's a good girl and she's grown into a beautiful woman. She's still odd, though."

"You're going to have to expand on that," Jared said. "She seemed normal to me."

"That's because you don't know her," Mel said. "This town is rife with stories about Harper Harlow. Ask anyone and you'll find people won't be able to shut up."

"Like?"

"She thinks she can see and talk to ghosts," Mel replied.

Whatever he was expecting his partner to say that wasn't it. Jared exhaled heavily, dumbfounded. "Excuse me?"

"It started when she was seven and her grandfather died," Mel explained. "She swore up and down he came into her room that night and told her he had to go away but would see her again."

"That's just a kid using her imagination."

"Her mother claims she was awake when she went in," Mel said. "That's not the only time it happened, though. There was an incident when she was in middle school and there were several incidents when she was in high school. After that … well … if you ask some people they believe Harper's claims."

"What do you believe?"

"I believe that she believes it and she's not trying to hurt anyone," Mel replied firmly. "I know Zander has faith that she has supernatural abilities. I would never call his belief in her into question. Trust me. He won't take it well. Those two are co-dependent and joined at the hip. They're loyal to each other above all else."

"This doesn't make sense to me," Jared said. "How can someone walk around and claim they talk to ghosts? Shouldn't her parents have gotten her therapy or something?"

"Her parents are a trip in their own right," Mel said. "They separated about a year ago and they're at war. I'm not sure they weren't at war their entire marriage. I have no idea how they stopped fighting long enough to even conceive Harper."

"Still, she should've been a priority to them," Jared argued. "They did her a disservice by letting her believe in that nonsense."

"What if it's not nonsense?"

"You just said you didn't believe it," Jared pointed out.

"I said I believe she believes it," Mel clarified. "I don't rightly know that she can't see ghosts. She has done a number of things that defy the impossible."

"Can you give me a for instance?"

"I've lost track of the number of bodies she's found," Mel said. "We're talking bodies that should've gone undiscovered for a long time without ... intervention. She found a girl who died at a kegger in high school. She also found a woman who slid off the road in a blizzard. The woman was dead, but her toddler wasn't and the little girl wouldn't have survived the night in that cold if Harper hadn't led us to her."

"That could be a coincidence," Jared suggested.

"It could be," Mel agreed. "Whatever it is Harper has turned it into a career for herself and she's taken Zander along for the ride."

"What career?"

Mel explained about Ghost Hunters, Inc., and when he was done Jared's mouth was hanging open.

"You have got to be kidding me," Jared said. "I cannot believe someone would actually hire the two of them to ... catch ghosts. That's unbelievable."

"It is," Mel said. "They make a decent living, though, and a lot of people swear by their work."

"How many ghosts could there possibly be in a town the size of Whisper Cove?" Jared's pragmatic mind was working overtime. "It has to be a scam."

"They don't always work in Whisper Cove," Mel said. "In fact, I would say the bulk of their jobs are in other towns. We're not too far from some very busy suburbs. My sister told me the two of them were out at Harsens Island earlier today clearing out Undercurrents."

"What's that?"

"It's a restaurant."

"And they kicked a ghost out of it?" Jared asked.

"They think they did," Mel said. "It's not for me to judge. I'm just telling you in case you run into the two of them around town. They might think our victim needs help."

"Oh, this is unbelievable," Jared said, running his hand through his dark hair. "How can you stand by and let them do this?"

"It's not my decision," Mel said. "I am not Zander's father and I'm certainly not in a power position when it comes to Harper. You might think she's crazy. Heck, I might think she's crazy. She's harmless, though. Just leave the two of them to their own devices."

"What if they get in the way of our investigation?" Jared pressed.

"Then we'll deal with that when it becomes an issue," Mel said. "For now, I think we need to identify our victim and move on from there."

Jared didn't argue with the suggestion or sentiment, but his mind was busy. How could a seemingly rational woman think she could see and talk to ghosts? There had to be more to the story.

FIVE

"They identified the victim," Zander said, sidling up to Harper's desk a few hours later. She'd been lost in thought – her gaze fixed on a far off location only she could see – since stumbling on the ghost after lunch. Zander knew she wasn't going to let her obsession go so he decided to help things along instead of fighting the process.

When Harper didn't immediately jump to her feet and start applauding his announcement Zander fixed her with a dark look. "Why thank you, Zander," he said, mimicking Harper's voice to perfection, years of close proximity fueling the uncanny impersonation. "I can't tell you how thankful I am that you went out of your way to get information for me."

Harper snapped her attention to Zander. "I was just thinking. I'm sorry I didn't give you the accolades you so richly deserve. You're the king, Zander."

"I know," Zander said, his tone smug. "It's nice to hear, though."

"I have no idea why I love you as much as I do," Harper said, rolling her eyes.

"It's because I'm handsome and witty."

"That's probably it," Harper conceded. "What is her name?"

"Annie Dresden," Zander said. "My mother talked to my uncle and he let it slip. All I know is that she was twenty-one and she wasn't from Whisper Cove."

"I think we both knew she wasn't from Whisper Cove," Harper said, rubbing the spot between her eyebrows. "We would've recognized anyone from town."

"Not if she was new."

"Whenever someone new comes to town it makes the weekly paper," Harper pointed out. "We knew the new cop was coming two weeks ago."

"Speaking of the new cop ... ." Zander broke off, eyeing the way Harper's shoulders straightened.

"What about him?"

Zander recognized the defensive tone of her voice. Since he hadn't said anything yet, he found her reaction ... interesting. "He's attractive, isn't he?" Zander asked, changing tactics. "Do you think he walks on my side of the street or your side of the street?"

"I really have no idea," Harper said, forcing her attention to her computer screen. "It's not any of my business."

"I'm hoping he walks on my side of the street," Zander said. "I would love to see what that stubble looks like in the morning if it's that ... rugged ... in the afternoon."

"Don't you think you should crash and burn with the waiter before you move on to the new cop?" Harper asked.

"I have plenty of time to do both," Zander said, shooting a charming wink at Harper. "I'm very good at multitasking."

"So you keep telling me," Harper said. "I don't believe it, though. If you're good at multitasking why can't you brush your teeth and shave at the same time without making a huge mess?"

"I do that so you can multitask," Zander replied, not missing a beat. "You like to clean while you're brushing your teeth."

"I only clean because you make a mess."

"If that's your story ... ."

Harper made a growling sound in the back of her throat. "Can we get back to the dead woman, please? We need to find out who Annie Dresden is and how she ended up out here."

"I can answer a little of that because I did some research online while my mom was going on and on about the new color of Aunt Shirley's hair," Zander said. "Mom says it looks like she could double for Ronald McDonald if their current mascot ever dies, by the way."

Harper snorted. "Aunt Shirley changes her hair color almost as much as Molly," she said. "What did you find on Annie?"

"Well, it's funny that you mentioned Molly," Zander said. "Annie is enrolled as a student at St. Clair Community College, just like our intrepid apprentice."

Harper's eyes widened. "Does Molly know Annie?"

Zander shrugged. "I have no idea," he said. "Molly is in class right now so we can't ask her. I looked at Annie's class schedule. She was focusing on business classes and our Molly is more of a ... free spirit. I'm not sure there's much of a crossover with the business and liberal arts students."

"That's probably true," Harper said. "Do you know where Annie was living?"

"I found an Annie Dresden that lives in a rental house in St. Clair," Zander said. "I think that's probably her."

"She didn't live on campus?"

"It's community college," Zander reminded her. "It's not like when we went to Central Michigan and almost everyone lived on campus ... well, at least the first two years."

"I guess that makes sense," Harper mused. "Do you know what I think?"

"I'm almost sure I do," Zander said. "You want to go to the campus and see if we can find someone who knew Annie. You're not going to sleep until you find out what happened to her and put her to rest. Do you know what that means for me?"

"I do," Harper said, getting to her feet. "It means you can't rest until I do. Let's go to the college."

"I knew you were going to say that," Zander muttered.

. . .

ST. CLAIR Community College was bustling with activity when Zander and Harper arrived. The students were milling about on campus, expensive coffees clutched in their hands, and they looked ... normal. They had no idea one of their own was gone – and possibly in a brutal way.

"It's almost time for finals," Zander said, watching the students with a happy grin. "Do you remember that feeling?"

"I remember dreading the tests," Harper replied, wrinkling her nose. "I hated the end of a semester."

"You hated the idea of going home to watch your parents fight," Zander corrected. "You liked the idea of getting a break from classes."

"You always have to be such a know-it-all."

"You love me anyway," Zander said, slinging an arm over Harper's shoulder. "Where do you want to start?"

As much as he irritated her Harper also found solace in Zander's presence. Even the simple act of putting an arm around her made her feel loved. "Do you know where the business classes are held here?"

"I've never actually been here," Zander admitted. "I've never had a reason."

"What about cruising for buff college students exploring their sexual identity?" Harper teased. "I would think that would be right up your alley."

"I never considered that before now," Zander replied, feigning interest. "It's like a buffet and I have an all-you-can-eat pass."

"You're sick."

"Seriously, where do you want to start?" Zander asked, his face sobering. "I can tell you're bothered by this. We should get to work."

"I'm bothered because she's a young woman who had her life cut short and she's obviously ... struggling ... with her new reality," Harper countered. "I think anyone would be bothered by that."

"I didn't say you were wrong to be bothered," Zander said. "I merely said I could tell you were bothered. Do you want to tell me what else is going on?"

Harper found herself on the defensive. "Who said anything else is going on?"

GHOSTLY INTERESTS

"You're acting ... weird," Zander said. "You were fine this morning even though you had horrendous bedhead and killer morning breath. You were in a good mood after we got paid at Undercurrents. You pouted throughout lunch, but that was mostly for show because you wanted to rain on my parade.

"Ever since we saw the ghost, though, you've been a morose pill," he continued. "I've had just about as much as I can swallow."

"No one said you had to come," Harper challenged.

"We both know that's not true," Zander said. "We're a set. Where you go, I go."

"Then stop complaining," Harper said. "And ... thank you. I love you."

"I love you, too," Zander said, pulling her in for a quick hug. "Now, point me in the direction of information and I shall glean it for you."

"Sometimes I think you missed your calling when you didn't stick to drama in college," Harper said. "That whole accounting degree you graduated with is completely wasted on you."

"If I didn't have that degree I wouldn't be able to run the business so smoothly."

"There is that," Harper said, rolling up on the balls of her feet and giving Zander a kiss on the cheek. "You're still a pain."

"I think that's one of the reasons we get along so well," Zander teased, tugging on a strand of her hair. "Come on. Let's do this. I'm starving."

"We just ate."

"I'm a growing boy and I need my nutrients," Zander replied, nonplussed. "I burn thousands of calories every day because my body is a temple."

"Does that mean you expect people to worship you?" Harper asked, cocking an eyebrow.

"You already worship me," Zander said. "You just don't want people to know it because you think it will hurt that women's lib thing you subscribe to."

"You're driving me crazy."

"Then we should get moving," Zander said. "A happily ever afterlife is beckoning Annie and we have to deliver it to her."

After studying the crowd for a few moments, Harper set her sights on a group of boisterous males cavorting in front of the university center. She approached them with a wide smile. "Um ... hi."

The man at the center of the group glanced at Harper, breaking into his own grin as he ran a hand through his blond hair. "Well, hello."

Harper fought to tamp down her irritation. This guy had "alpha" written all over him. She was a fan of testosterone. She wasn't a fan of men who thought that excused bad behavior. "I don't suppose we could ask a few questions, could we?"

"You can ask me anything you want, sweetheart," the man said. "Before you ask the obvious question, though, I'll answer it for you. Yes, I am well endowed."

Harper made a face as Zander moved up to her side. He was an impressive mass of muscle and even though he wasn't prone to fits of violence he also wasn't apt to ignore anyone talking crudely to his best friends. "I've found that most men who are well endowed don't find the need to announce it," Zander said.

"Maybe that's because you shop in the pink section," the man sneered.

"I do love pink," Zander said, unruffled. "I'm betting I know what I'm talking about more than you do, though."

Harper put a hand on Zander's arm to still him. "There's no reason to Hulk out," she said. "He's just looking for attention. It's okay."

"I get plenty of attention," the man said.

"Knock it off, Jay." One of the other men, this one shorter and darker, took a step forward. "I apologize for my brother's behavior. The spring weather makes him ... crazy."

"I was going to say horny," Zander said dryly.

"That, too," the second man said. "I'm Collin Graham, by the way. This is my brother Jay."

"It's nice to meet you," Harper said, extending her hand to shake Collin's. "I see bad manners don't run in your family."

"Neither does being well endowed," Jay sniped, puffing his chest out.

Harper ignored him and focused on Collin. "We're here to ask some questions about a student who attends classes here," she said. "Her name is Annie Dresden. Do you know her?"

Collin smiled amiably. "Sure. I know Annie. She's in a few of my business classes."

"She's hot, too," Jay said. "I would totally hit that." He mimed a sexual act behind his brother's back.

"Is she in trouble?" Collin asked.

"She's dead," Harper replied, her voice even.

Collin's previously placid face drained of color as he ran a hand through his muddy hair. "Are you serious?"

Even Jay had the grace to look abashed. "No way."

"She was found in Whisper Cove today," Harper said. "Her body was on the beach. Did she have ties to that area?"

"I have no idea," Collin said. "I didn't know her all that well. We had a few classes together … and were friendly … but we didn't hang out or anything."

"What do you know about her?"

"That's a very good question. I'm most interested in hearing why Ms. Harlow is here asking it."

Harper froze when she heard the voice behind her and when she stiffly turned she found Jared Monroe watching her from a few feet away.

"Oh, crap."

SIX

Jared's eyes were a clear shade of blue and Harper could almost feel the icy cold emanating from them as they bore into her.

"What are you doing here?" Jared asked, crossing his arms over his chest as he regarded her. Next to him Mel was silently shaking his head and rolling his eyes.

"We're ... hanging out," Harper answered, shifting uncomfortably.

"You're hanging out with college kids?" Jared pressed. "That makes me feel a little uncomfortable. Are you running out of people to date in Whisper Cove?"

Harper scowled. "No. That's not what we were doing."

"What *were* you doing?" Jared asked.

"I ... ." Harper broke off, unsure how to answer. She had no idea why Jared's mere presence unnerved her, but it did.

"I knew I shouldn't have told your mother we identified the victim," Mel said, shooting Zander a dark look. "She told you, didn't she?"

"Why would she do that?" Jared asked.

"Because she can never tell her son no," Mel said. "How did you know I would tell her?"

"Because I know you," Zander said. "Mom is gossipy and you like to gossip with her. This is the biggest thing to hit Whisper Cove in years. There's no way you don't want to talk about it. I played a hunch."

"Did you have to hear about Shirley's hair, too?"

"Ronald McDonald better start looking over his shoulder."

Jared wasn't nearly as entertained by the repartee as Harper. "You told a civilian about our murder victim?"

Mel shrugged, nonplussed. "So what? It's not like it's a secret."

"When did you tell her? Was it before or after we notified her parents? You remember the people who broke down in tears and sobbed for twenty minutes, right?"

Mel swallowed hard. "It was before," he said. "If you think I'm not taking this seriously you're wrong. It's just ... she asked. People are going to be talking about this. Whisper Cove is tiny. People want to know what's going on. You'll find that out."

"Whatever," Jared said, scowling. "Nancy Drew, Joe Hardy, if you will? I think we can take it from here."

Harper placed her hands on her narrow hips. "Nancy Drew? If I'm anyone it's Trixie Belden."

Jared was taken aback. It wasn't the response he was expecting. "I ... who is Trixie Belden?"

"Oh, man, don't cite the genre if you can't hold up your end of the argument," Zander said, wagging his finger in Jared's direction.

"I have no idea what that means, but you're starting to bug me," Jared said.

"They weren't doing anything," Collin piped in. "They were just asking questions about Annie. We had no idea anything happened to her."

Jared exchanged introductions with the group, occasionally glancing at Harper and Zander but otherwise ignoring them. "Did you know Annie?"

"Only on a superficial level," Collin said.

"Meaning?"

"We had a couple of classes together," Collin replied. "We were friendly but not close."

"I wanted to be close with her," Jay said, winking at Harper. "She missed out, but it's not too late for that sweet blonde over there."

Jared shot him a dark look. "Are you seriously trying to pick up a woman while we're questioning you about the death of one of your classmates?"

Jay's face flooded with color. "I ... ."

"Don't bother coming up with an excuse," Jared chided. "There is no excuse. Besides, she's old enough to be your ... ."

"Don't you dare even think of finishing that sentence," Harper warned.

"I was going to say older sister."

"No, you weren't. Don't lie. We both know you were going to say something else. And, just so you know, I happen to be two years younger than you," Harper said.

"How do you know how old I am?"

"Because Whisper Cove could fit on the head of a pin," Harper replied. "We all know each other's business."

"Well, in that case, I would appreciate it if you took your business over there so I can question these fine, upstanding citizens without an audience," Jared said.

"Why can't I stay here?" Harper pressed.

"Because I said so."

"But ... ."

"Zander, enough is enough," Mel said. "Take Harper and do ... whatever it is you two do. This isn't one of your fun little cases. This is official police business and it's serious."

"Little cases?" Now Zander was the irritated one. "I'll have you know ... ."

"Come on," Harper said, grabbing his arm and tugging so she could lead Zander away from Jared and the college boys. "It's not worth it. We'll find our own people to interview."

"Fine," Zander said. "This isn't over, though. I'm calling Mom when I get home and she's going to have more than Aunt Shirley's hair color on her lips when she calls you tonight."

Mel visibly deflated. "I can't wait."

"That's what you get for messing with your favorite nephew," Zander shot back.

AS LUCK WOULD HAVE it Zander and Harper didn't have to wander far to find new college students to question. Once they turned the corner of the university center they found Molly's familiar face, and she was the center of attention as she regaled her classmates.

Harper approached her, and when Molly recognized her surprise washed over her face. "I ... what are you doing here? Is something wrong?"

"Nothing is wrong," Harper said. "I ... well ... it's hard to explain why we're here."

"A student named Annie Dresden was found dead on the beach out by Lake St. Clair," Zander said. "Harper is obsessed with finding out how she died and how she ended up out there. We know she was a student here. We're trying to find someone who knew her."

"Apparently it's not that hard to explain," Harper said.

"Annie Dresden?" Molly furrowed her brow. "I'm not sure I know her."

"She was tall and willowy," Harper explained. "She was a business major."

"Well, that would explain that," Molly said. "I don't hang around with the business students. They're far too serious."

"Oh, don't say that," Collin said, sidling up beside Harper and smiling at Molly. "Just because we want to learn how to make a lot of money doesn't mean we don't want to have fun, too."

"Did you follow me?" Harper asked, shifting her attention to Collin.

"The mean cop said he didn't have any other questions for me and let me go," Collin said, shrugging. "I saw you over here with your friend. I never got a chance to properly apologize for what my brother said to you over there so I thought I would do it now."

"It's not your fault that your brother is a jerkwad," Harper said, patting Collin's shoulder. "You were perfectly pleasant. That's all that matters. You can't hold yourself accountable for other people's actions."

"If that's true how come you always apologize to the grocery clerk when I hold up the cantaloupes to my chest and ask you to squeeze my melons?" Zander asked.

"Because that's just ... not funny," Harper replied.

"Says you," Zander grumbled. "I happen to think it's very funny."

"And that's why you're not allowed to go to the farmer's market in the summer without an escort," Harper shot back.

Molly smirked at Zander and Harper's antics. She was used to them. Her flirty eyes were fixed on Collin, though. "I've seen you around," she said. "You're always with that blond boy with the bad attitude, right?"

"My brother," Collin said. "If he's ever said anything inappropriate to you, I apologize."

"He just asked to touch my melons," Molly joked, leaning closer to Collin and twirling her bobbed hair around her finger.

Harper wasn't great on picking up body language, but Molly's was obvious. She was interested in Collin. Unfortunately, while Collin looked friendly, his interest in the fuchsia-haired siren was hard to read.

"We should get going," Harper said. "Molly, I'll see you at work. Collin, it was very nice to meet you."

"You, too."

Zander followed Harper, surprised to find her moving back in the direction of the university center. "Where are we going?"

"I'm playing a hunch."

"What hunch?"

"I'm going to hide in the bushes and see if I can listen to Officer Stick-Up-His-Butt and see if he finds anything out."

"Is that really a good idea?" Zander wasn't thrilled at the prospect.

"Probably not. I'm still going to do it. No one says you have to come."

"We've already been over this," Zander said. "We're a team. Just for the record, though, you really are Trixie Belden."

"And don't you forget it."

"YOU SAW Annie around campus but never had the occasion to talk to her? Is that what you're saying?" Jared's patience with Jay was starting to wear thin. While his brother was open and cordial, Jay was displaying at least three diagnosable personality disorders – and narcissism was the most pleasant one.

"I talked to her a few times," Jay conceded.

"Did you ask her out?"

"You don't really date in college," Jay said, talking down to Jared as if he was a pitiable older gentleman who wasn't quick on the uptake when it came to the comings and goings of a younger generation. "You hook up and then turn it out."

"Did you hook up with Annie?" Jared asked, fighting the urge to roll his eyes. He almost wished he'd left Harper to her questions when it came to this guy. If he spent five more minutes with him he was going to have to throttle him just to put an end to the drivel trickling out of his mouth.

"She wanted to, but she also wanted to make me beg for it and Jay Graham doesn't beg."

He apparently talked about himself in the third person, though, Jared internally mused. "In other words you asked her out and she said no," he said. "Did you just let it go or did you try to force the issue?"

Jay finally registered an emotion and it was disbelief. "I don't force anything," he said. "People beg for the privilege to hang out with me. I don't beg them for anything. I don't have to. I'm very popular."

"That won't last very long," Jared muttered.

"Excuse me?" Jay was back to being full of himself.

"Trust me. Once you're out of a closed environment like this you're going to find out that the only one you impress with that attitude is yourself."

"I don't have to take this," Jay grumbled.

"I'm almost done," Jared said. "All I want to know is if you ever saw Annie on campus with anyone who would strike you as suspicious."

"I don't know where you hang out, but most people don't wear their 'I'm a murderer' shirts in public here," Jay replied.

"Is that a no?"

"Well ... ." Jay broke off, chewing on his bottom lip as he considered how to answer.

"We're not going to arrest someone just because you pointed us in their direction," Jared said.

"I did see her with someone a couple of times," Jay conceded. "At first I thought they were talking about class assignments but then ... well ... I saw them down by the pond and they were making out."

"What is this student's name?"

"That's the thing, he's not a student," Jay said. "He's a professor."

Jared's interest was genuinely piqued now. "What's this professor's name?"

"Michael Dalton," Jay answered. "He teaches a few economics classes and one business advertising course."

"How many times did you see him with Annie?"

"At least three times," Jay said.

"Can you point us in the direction of the business building?" Jared asked.

Jay did as instructed.

Jared thanked him for his time and as he was about to turn and leave Jay pulled his attention back to him.

"If you could leave out the part of this where I'm the one who told you about Professor Dalton's relationship with Annie that would be great," Jay said.

"Why is that?"

"He's my professor and I really want to pass."

Jared smirked. He hated the guy and yet he understood his plight.

"Don't worry. Your secret is safe with us. No one will know where the information came from."

As Jared moved past the thick grove of bushes he didn't look behind the purple blooms. If he had he would have seen Harper and Zander exchanging excited looks.

"Well done, Trixie Belden," Zander whispered. "I'll never doubt your spying skills again."

SEVEN

Professor Michael Dalton was surprised to find two police officers standing outside of his office when he opened the door. Jared tried to gauge the man from a few feet away, but the only emotion he saw reflected on the handsome instructor's face was shock.

Jared could see why a twenty-one-year-old woman would be attracted to the man. At thirty-five years of age, he was young enough to retain all of the physical attributes associated with youth and yet he was still old enough to give off an air of maturity.

For some reason, Jared didn't like him on sight. "We hate to bother you, Professor Dalton, but we have a matter of some urgency to discuss with you."

"My office hours are over with for the day," Dalton said, running a hand through his brown hair. It was long enough to give him that "dangerous" look women love so much and yet well maintained so people didn't mistake him for a student. "I will have open hours again between noon and two tomorrow."

Jared had to give the guy credit. He was surprised by the appearance of police officers and yet he wasn't ceding his power position without a fight.

"We're not here to talk about your curriculum, sir," Mel said, exchanging an amused look with Jared. "We're here on official business and it doesn't include whatever textbook you're hawking in your class."

Dalton scowled. "All you had to do was say that your questions couldn't wait," he said. "There's no reason to be jerks."

"I wasn't aware we were being jerks," Jared replied, his immovable cop face in place. "Can we come inside?"

"I guess." Dalton was resigned.

Once everyone was settled, Jared cut right to the chase. "Professor Dalton, it has come to our attention that you have a romantic relationship with one of your students," he said.

"That's not against the law."

"I didn't say it was against the law," Jared said, tugging on his limited patience. "We need some information about your relationship ...."

"It's no one's business who I'm dating," Dalton said, cutting Jared off before he could finish his sentence. "No one here is underage. Everyone here can legally consent. I don't understand why you guys are making such a big deal about this. Did Jackie complain or something?"

Jared faltered, confused at the shift in the conversation. He took a moment to regroup and then plowed on. "Professor Dalton, no one cares that you're dating a student. I have no idea who Jackie is. We're here to talk to you about Annie Dresden."

"Annie?" Dalton leaned back in his chair, rubbing the back of his neck as he realized Jared and Mel were in his office for something other than what he was expecting. "What about Annie? She didn't show up for class today."

"You dated her, right?"

"I don't think that 'date' is the right word," Dalton said. "We spent a little time together. We were never officially a couple. Is Annie saying I did something to her or something? If so, you should know she didn't take the fact that I didn't want a relationship with her very well and she threatened to make a scene because she said I broke her heart."

That was a lot of information to absorb and Jared wasn't sure where to start with his next round of questions. "Are you saying you're not currently involved with Annie Dresden?"

"We were never involved," Dalton said. "I just told you that."

"Sir, we have witnesses who saw you kissing Annie down by the pond," Jared said. He had no idea why the man was lying, but Jared was on alert. Something else was going on here.

"So what? I said we weren't dating," Dalton said. "I never said we didn't have sex."

Jared was floored by the instructor's cavalier attitude. "Excuse me?"

As if sensing that Jared's temper was about to get the better of him Mel stepped in smoothly. "Sir, when did your sexual relationship with Miss Dresden end?"

"I don't know," Dalton said. "We had sex four times. When she called to ask me to dinner I declined and explained I was going out with someone else and she flipped out."

"Do you date a lot of your students?" Jared asked, a nerve ticking in his tight jaw.

"I don't think 'date' is the right word," Dalton said.

Jared was at his wit's end. "Sir, I don't know if you're trying to play a game here, but I'm in no mood to put up with any of … this."

"You came to me," Dalton reminded him.

"I'm not interested in rephrasing questions to get them semantically right," Jared said. "I want to know how long you dated Annie Dresden and when the last time you saw her was. Period."

"I'm also interested in how many of your students you date at once," Mel added.

Dalton was surprised by Jared's vehemence. "I … don't know. I told you we slept together a few times. Annie thought we were embarking on a relationship. When I told her that wasn't the case she accused me of using her and had a fit."

"How did you respond?" Mel asked.

"I suggested that taking someone else's class next semester would probably be the smartest way to go."

"When was the last time you saw her?" Jared asked.

"Um ... I'm going to say the day before yesterday," Dalton said. "She was in class, but we didn't speak. She gave me some dirty looks and I ignored them. She was being pretty pathetic, if you ask me. It's not like we were in love or anything."

Jared fought the urge to punch the man. His blasé attitude was beyond grating. "Where were you last night?"

While the medical examiner was still working on Annie's body he did provide Mel and Jared with a few tidbits to start their investigation besides her identification. He put the time of death around 10 p.m. the previous evening and said she was dead before she hit the water. The other details would take more time.

"I ... what is this about?" Dalton asked.

"Answer the question," Jared ordered.

"Not until you tell me what this is about," Dalton replied, holding firm.

"Annie Dresden was found dead on the beach in Whisper Cove today," Mel supplied. "We need to know your whereabouts last evening, sir."

"Oh, my ... ." Dalton looked genuinely shocked. "I ... how did she die?"

"We're still working that out," Mel said. "We need to know where you were last night."

"I was at home."

"Can anyone verify that?" Jared asked.

Dalton narrowed his eyes until they were dangerous slits. "What exactly are you insinuating?"

"I'm not insinuating anything," Jared countered. "I'm trying to ascertain if you have a witness to your alibi."

"I was alone," Dalton said, crossing his arms over his chest and releasing a shaky sigh.

"What about this Jackie?" Mel pressed. "Were you with her?"

"I was on campus until about six and then I went home," Dalton said. "I was alone. I don't have a witness and I don't need one because I didn't do anything."

"Is this like when you weren't dating Annie?" Jared asked, his belligerence getting the better of him.

"You know what? I think we're done here," Dalton said, his tone shifting from nervous to angry. "I don't have to tell you anything. I'm an innocent man. You can get out of my office right now."

"We still have questions," Jared argued.

"Take them up with my lawyer," Dalton spat. "We're done."

"THIS IS ALL SO CREEPY," Molly said, her eyes wide after Zander finished catching her up on the day's events. "Do we know how she died yet?"

Despite her interest in Collin, and his half-hearted invitation to a party, Molly begged off and let her curiosity drag her back to the GHI offices. She had to know how Zander and Harper were drawn into Annie Dresden's murder investigation.

"I don't know if the cops even know how she died yet," Zander said. "We only got Annie's identification because my mother bugged Mel until he gave it up. I don't think that's going to happen again since the new cop was not happy when he found out."

"He's a tool," Harper said, her gaze focused on her computer screen as she followed Annie's digital footprint on Facebook.

"I think you like him," Zander teased.

"Who does Harper like?" Eric asked, strolling into the office. He gave the appearance of being relaxed, but Zander could read the rigid set of his shoulders from five feet away.

"The new cop," Zander said. He felt bad for Eric, but it was never going to happen with Harper. No matter how long the man lusted after his best friend she was never going to return the feelings. Jared Monroe was another matter entirely. While Whisper Cove's newest police officer was prickly he was also attractive, and whether Harper realized it or not, she was reacting to Jared in a way she probably didn't comprehend.

"How did you meet the new cop already?" Eric asked.

Instead of giving Zander a chance to answer Molly did it for him. If Eric's crush on Harper was unrequited, Molly's crush on Eric was eternally doomed. She didn't see it, just like Eric didn't see his crush was never going to be returned. When Molly was done Eric was flabbergasted.

"How come nobody ever comes to get me for these little outings?" Eric asked.

"Harper and I were eating lunch when it happened," Zander replied. "When we came back to the office you weren't here. She wanted to go to the campus right away. What were we supposed to do?"

"Have you heard about these newfangled cell phone contraptions?" Eric pulled his out of his pocket and waved it in Zander's face for emphasis.

"No," Zander said, turning his attention back to Molly. "We need you to keep your ears open on campus. If you hear anyone talking about Annie, find out how well they know her and anything else they can tell us about her day-to-day activities."

"We already know she was dating a professor," Harper added.

"She was?" Molly perked up. "Which professor?"

"Michael Dalton."

Molly's interest waned. "I wouldn't get too excited about him," she said. "Rumor has it that he'll date anything with the right parts. He's not particular. He has sex with any co-ed who even smiles at him. He's got quite the reputation as a ladies man. I think he's the one who spreads those rumors, though, because he likes people to think of him as some un-gettable lothario."

"You just said he was gettable," Harper pointed out.

"Fine. You're right," Molly conceded. "Getting him isn't the problem. Keeping him for more than three or four rolls in the hay is the problem."

"If everyone knows about his reputation, why does the college keep him on?" Zander asked.

"He's hot," Molly said. "His classes always fill up, so as long as no formal complaints are filed against him, he's golden."

"That's just … wrong," Harper said, making a face. "If he's notorious on campus, though, I'm not sure what his motive for killing Annie would be. It doesn't sound like they were serious."

"Probably not from his end," Molly said. "I know several girls have gotten their noses out of joint about being dumped by Dalton, though. Everyone thinks they're going to be the one to tame him and they take it rough when it doesn't happen."

"The motive is in what Molly just told us," Zander pointed out.

Harper furrowed her brow. "It is? I must have missed it."

"Well, *Trixie Belden*, Molly said that Dalton gets away with dating his students as long as no formal complaints are filed," Zander said. "Maybe Annie threatened to file a complaint because of the way he dumped her in the dirt."

The theory intrigued Harper. "That's a good point," she said, rubbing her index finger against her cheek thoughtfully. "That does give him a pretty solid motive."

"It does," Zander agreed. "What we need to do is find out what Dalton's status with Annie was at the time of her death."

"We also need a firm time of death," Harper added.

"I'll call my mom and have her bug Uncle Mel for whatever tidbits she can glean tonight," Zander said. "Molly, your mission is to find out whatever dirt you can on Dalton. Find out who he is sleeping with now and see if you can find any exes who will be willing to talk to us."

Molly clicked her heels together and mock saluted. Despite her reaction, the excitement on her face was obvious. "This is going to be so much fun," she said. "It's like we're detectives."

"We're like Sherlock and Watson," Zander agreed.

"We're more like Scooby-Doo," Eric said.

Zander pondered the thought. "That means Molly is Thelma, Harper is Daphne, you're Shaggy, and I'm Fred."

"I'm Fred," Eric corrected.

"Who wants to be Fred?" Harper asked. "He dressed like an idiot and he was clearly gay. Oh, wait, that means Zander is definitely Fred."

"I told you," Zander said, winking at Eric triumphantly.

"I don't want to be Shaggy," Eric argued.

"Then you're Scooby-Doo," Zander said. "I love it. Do you want a Scooby-Snack?"

"How did I end up being a dog in this scenario?" Eric was frustrated.

"We all have our lots in life," Harper replied. "Now everyone get to work. We need to do some research and the best way to do it is going to be at the candlelight vigil on campus tonight."

"There's a candlelight vigil?" Molly asked. "How do you know that?"

"Someone posted it on Facebook," Harper said. "That's where we're starting so everyone get your dinner and gear up because we have a murder to solve and a ghost to put to rest."

"She might be more Thelma than me," Molly said.

"No, she's Shaggy," Zander said, tousling Harper's hair affectionately. "All she's missing is the constant pot buzz and shower aversion."

EIGHT

"Does anyone else find candlelight vigils creepy?" Eric asked a few hours later.

The St. Clair Community College campus was buzzing with activity, word of Annie's death spreading like wildfire. While the police weren't releasing a cause of death, the student population was already passing news of Annie's brutal murder along as if it was fact. Harper had a feeling they were right, but she didn't like it when people jumped to conclusions.

"How are they creepy?" Molly asked, her gaze focused on the spot in front of the administration building where people were placing roses before the ceremony. "I think it's nice. People want to mourn the loss of their friend."

"That's just it," Eric said. "Are we really supposed to believe all of these people were Annie's friends? I can't help but feel some of them are here because they like the spectacle of death and want to be a part of something ... big."

"That's pretty jaded," Molly chided.

"I think it's realistic."

Molly and Eric turned to Harper expectantly, as if she was their mother and the deciding factor in their little argument. "I think you're both right," Harper said. "I think that whenever death hits young people they can't help but react because they see themselves as untouchable and someone their age being taken before their time jars them."

Molly stuck her tongue out in Eric's direction.

"I also think a lot of these people showed up because there's a ghoulish factor to media-covered deaths," Harper said, pointing at the television reporters as they set up on the other side of the action. "People want to be where the excitement is. I'm sure a lot of these people have no idea who Annie is and they don't really care because they're more worried about whether or not they can get on television."

Eric sneered at Molly as she deflated.

"I think it's a mixture of people," Harper said. "Like all things in life there are good and bad aspects of death and the way people react to it."

"Are you in fortune cookie mode tonight?" Zander teased.

"I'm merely waxing poetic," Harper shot back. She clapped her hands together to draw everyone's attention away from the spectacle and back to her. "I want everyone to split up and see what they can find out. Don't wander too far away and Molly, if you see this professor, come and find me. I'm dying to meet him."

"Will do."

JAY GRAHAM WAS HOLDING court amidst his fan club when he caught sight of Harper. She was winding through the crowd and she looked lost in thought. He didn't care what the dour cop said about how old she was. He liked what he saw and older women were better to play with because they knew what they were doing and were often grateful for the attention from a young stud like himself.

He told his friends he would be back in a few minutes, winked at two girls who had been trying to flirt with him all night, and then started moving in Harper's direction. He didn't want to alienate the girls in case he struck out with Harper. He was definitely more interested in her, though.

"Where are you going?" Collin asked, stepping into his brother's path.

"That hot blonde from earlier today is over there," Jay said, pointing. "I want to talk to her."

"She's way out of your league."

"No one is out of my league," Jay countered.

"She is."

"We'll just see about that."

"ARE you sure this was a good idea?" Mel asked Jared, furrowing his brow as he studied the candlelight vigil crowd, which was growing by the minute. "There are too many people here to get a feeling for any one suspect."

"I'm not interested in questioning anyone," Jared said.

"Then why are we here?"

"Because I want to see if anyone out of the ordinary shows up."

"Like?"

"I don't know," Jared said, shrugging. "I'm looking for anyone who doesn't look like he should be here. Some killers get off on watching public displays of mourning when it comes to their victims."

"We don't technically know that Annie was a victim of anything," Mel reminded him. "The medical examiner said he wouldn't complete his findings until tomorrow morning."

"Don't get me started on that," Jared warned. "Doesn't it bother you that it's taking so long?"

Mel shrugged. "We're not big enough to have our own medical examiner," he said. "The county has twelve communities that utilize their services when it comes to suspicious bodies. The guy can only do what he can do."

"Well, it bothers me," Jared said.

"Partner, from what I can tell, pretty much everything bothers you," Mel said. "You might want to lay off the caffeine. You're a little intense."

"Whatever," Jared said, rolling his eyes. "I think we should split up and look around. If you see anything suspicious ... ."

"I'll call you and let you handle it," Mel said, fighting to tamp his irritation down. "Lord knows I could never do my job without you."

Jared ignored the sarcasm. "I'm going to start over there."

HARPER WATCHED the students with a trained eye and heavy heart. Some of them were genuinely upset. She could ignore the outliers because she understood their need to be a part of this, but she truly felt for the students struggling with the questions of mortality and what lived beyond the human veil.

She was so lost in thought she didn't notice a shadowy figure moving in on her until it was already upon her. She jumped when she turned, finding Molly's eager face mere inches from her own.

"You scared the crap out of me," Harper said, lifting her hand to her heart. "Don't do that."

"I'm sorry," Molly said. "I thought I would come and see how you were doing. I'm not having much luck. Some people are really upset, but no one knows of any enemies Annie had or how she ended up in Whisper Cove. As far as I can tell she didn't have any ties to the community."

"What have you found out?"

"Her parents live in Sterling Heights and she attended Utica High School," Molly said. "She seemed well liked and other than her stupid decision to sleep with Professor Dalton she wasn't known as much of a dater."

"Well, that's disappointing," Harper said. "I was hoping we would get a few leads."

"Can I ask why this is so important to you?" Molly asked. "Is it because you were the first person she saw once she realized she was ... dead?"

"It's because she looked lost and I want to make sure she's found before everyone forgets her," Harper replied. "I ... I don't know why I can do the things I do. I believe I'm meant to help people, though. If I can't help Annie then what good are my abilities?"

"You've helped a lot of spirits move on," Molly reminded her earnestly. "It's not possible to help everyone."

"I know that," Harper said, her face softening. "For some reason I really want to help Annie, though. I can't explain it."

"Then we should help Annie," Molly said. "You'll figure it out. You always do. I have faith."

Harper gripped Molly's hand briefly. "Thank you."

"Now that's what I like to see. I love it when two hot women pet each other in public."

Harper stiffened when she heard the voice, swiveling her shoulders until her eyes met Jay's predatory gaze. "Why am I not surprised to see you?"

"I think you were secretly wishing for it," Jay said, winking.

"I think you're delusional," Harper replied.

"You're Collin's brother, aren't you?" Molly asked, dragging Jay's attention away from Harper. "I've seen you on campus. Your brother told me you two spend a lot of time together."

"How do you know Collin?" Jay asked.

"We met on campus today."

"You go to school here?" Jay looked surprised. "I find that hard to believe."

"And why is that?" Molly asked, her hands on her hips as she leaned forward. "Do you think a woman with pink streaks in her hair can't pass a college course?" She was used to people underestimating her, but that didn't mean she liked it.

"No," Jay said, holding his hands up in a placating manner. "I just meant that I would've remembered seeing someone as hot as you on this campus. I wasn't trying to offend you."

"Oh," Molly said, marginally relaxing. "I ... um ... sorry."

"Don't worry about it," Jay said, chuckling. "I like fiery women."

Harper rolled her eyes until they landed on another familiar figure. It looked as if Collin was coming to see what sort of hijinks his brother was involved in. "Hi."

Collin returned Harper's greeting with a shy smile. "Hi. Um ... my brother isn't doing anything horrible, is he?"

"Of course not," Jay said, glaring at his brother. "You don't always need to make excuses for me. You know that, right?"

"I wasn't making excuses."

"Well ... don't."

"I'm going to leave you guys to chat," Harper said, fixing her pointed gaze on Molly. "I'm going to look around. I'll see you in a little bit."

Since Molly was more interested in Collin than the murder investigation she merely nodded distractedly. "Yeah. I'll be right behind you."

Harper was halfway across the administration building's expansive lawn when a student caught her attention.

"Hi, Professor Dalton."

Harper snapped her head in the direction of the voice and followed the gaze of the waving brunette. When her gaze landed on the professor, who was returning the gesture, she realized why Dalton was so popular with the female student body. He was definitely attractive. She squared her shoulders and changed her direction, moving for Dalton with a purpose – and what she hoped was a friendly smile. If he thought she was up to something, her approach would be over before it even began.

"Hi," Harper said, stepping into Dalton's path. "Are you with the faculty here?"

"I am," Dalton said, looking Harper up and down with hungry eyes. "Are you a student here? Surely not. I think I would remember you."

"I'm not a student," Harper said. "I'm here because I heard the news and felt horrible for this poor woman."

"Yeah, it's a tragedy," Dalton said, rubbing the back of his neck. "Whenever a student dies I can't help but wonder how God could take someone so young and leave so many wretched people behind."

He was trying to be profound, but Harper could see right through him. "Yes. It is awful. Did you know her?"

"I knew her in class."

"Was she a good student?" Harper pressed.

"They're all good students."

This was getting her nowhere. Harper realized that. Dalton was so used to playing games that he couldn't stop himself from doing it in the midst of a real tragedy. "When did you and Annie break up?" The words were out of her mouth before Harper had time to think better of them.

Dalton narrowed his eyes. "Who told you that?"

"Everyone on campus knows," Harper said. "It wasn't a secret. You're notorious for loving and leaving co-eds at every turn."

"Are you jealous?" Dalton asked, reaching over and rubbing his index finger up and down Harper's bare forearm. "You don't have to be. You're a little older than I like, but you do have certain ... attributes ... I find appealing." His eyes roved over Harper's rounded rear. "Very appealing."

Harper yanked her arm back. "I don't think you're my type."

"I think you're selling yourself short," Dalton said. "I don't really have a type."

"I think you misheard me," Harper said, her voice firm. "You're not my type. I don't give a rat's behind if I'm your type."

"Oh, now, don't be like that," Dalton said, smiling wolfishly. "I think you would like what I have to offer."

"And I think she's already turned you down," Jared said, moving between Harper and Dalton and forcing the instructor to take an involuntary step back.

Harper sucked in a breath, surprised at Jared's appearance and reaction to Dalton. "I ... we were just talking."

"Oh, I knew what you were doing, Trixie Belden," Jared said, his eyes never leaving Dalton's face. "I'm not sure if you know what this guy was doing."

"I'm not a child," Harper said. "I know what he was doing. I was trying to get some information out of him about Annie. That's all."

Jared finally moved his gaze from Dalton's fearful eyes to Harper's obstinate blue orbs. "Why are you looking for information on Annie?"

"I'm curious."

"I'm going to be going," Dalton said, his gaze bouncing between Harper and Jared. "I ... have a nice night."

"I have more questions, Professor," Jared called to his rapidly retreating back. "Would you like to answer them?"

"I already told you to go through my lawyer."

"That's what I thought you would say," Jared grumbled, watching Dalton for a few moments before turning his attention to Harper. "Do you want to tell me what you're really doing here?"

"Mourning the loss of a young woman who was cut down in her prime," Harper replied, not missing a beat.

"I see." Jared was fighting to tamp down the smile threatening the corners of his mouth. He hated amateurs getting involved in official investigations and yet there was something about Harper that amused him. She had a goofy charm that he couldn't put a name to and yet still found appealing. "Are you staying for the whole vigil?"

Harper shrugged. "Maybe. Are you?"

"Maybe," Jared said, his face unreadable as he studied her. "Are you here because you think you're helping Annie's ghost?"

Harper was floored by the question. "Who told you that?"

"Mel mentioned that you and Zander run a ghost busting business," Jared said. "I've been trying to figure out why you're so interested in Annie and the only thing I can come up with is that you've convinced yourself that she's a ghost."

"I've convinced myself?" Harper arched a confrontational eyebrow. "That's some bedside manner you've got there, Doctor."

"I'm not trying to offend you," Jared said. "I'm trying to figure out your angle. Do you convince people they have ghosts or do they convince themselves of that and conveniently find you?"

"I get that you don't believe in ghosts, but there's no reason to make fun of my beliefs," Harper said.

"I'm not making fun of your beliefs ... especially because I'm doubtful that you believe any of this ... but I can't figure out how this works and I'm dying to know how you managed to convince people that you can see and talk to ghosts," Jared said.

"Not everyone has a limited outlook on life," Harper snapped.

"If you don't want to answer me you don't have to," Jared said. "Like I said, I'm curious."

"You're not curious," Harper countered. "You've convinced yourself of who I am and what I'm doing without any facts or listening to any other arguments besides the judgmental conga line in your head."

Jared's mouth dropped open, stunned by her fortitude.

"I don't care what you believe," Harper said. "I don't care if you think I'm the fruitiest loop in the box. I know who I am and what I can do and I'm not about to let the likes of you bring me down."

"Wait just a minute," Jared said.

"No," Harper replied, shaking her head. "We can agree to disagree. I am not going to change your belief system and you're certainly not going to change mine. We can both go our separate ways and no one has to have their feelings hurt."

"I think I might've already hurt your feelings and that's not what I meant to do," Jared said.

"You didn't hurt my feelings," Harper replied. "You're not capable of it. Meaner men have tried. You can trust me there."

"I ...."

Harper shook her head, cutting him off. "I need to find Zander and I'm sure you need to find Mel," she said. "Have a good evening, Officer Monroe."

"Ms. Harlow ... ."

Harper was already walking away before Jared could offer whatever half-hearted apology was on the tip of his tongue. "Oh, and Officer Monroe?"

Jared lifted a quizzical eyebrow, trying hard to focus on her face and not her shapely lower body even though it was swinging in a tantalizing way as she stormed off.

"You're a big douche," Harper said, turning back around and disappearing into the crowd.

Jared scowled as he watched her go. "What just happened here?"

NINE

"I need this ghost gone and I need it gone today." Nina Jackson was matter-of-fact as she regarded Zander and Harper the next morning. "I know you charge a premium fee for fast jobs and I'm willing to pay it if you can get this ghost out of here today."

Zander and Harper exchanged a look.

"You have to sign a contract before we do it," Zander said. "We don't expect payment before we complete the job, but we do expect the promise of payment for when it's done."

"Whatever," Nina said, waving her hand impatiently. "I'm willing to pay any fee to get this ghost out of here."

"I'll get the forms out of the car," Zander said. "I'll call our co-workers and get them out here. While I'm doing that, you should tell Harper what you can about this ghost."

Nina made a face. "Why?"

"Because it will help us form the best plan of attack," Harper replied smoothly.

"Can't you just ... I don't know ... suck it up?" Nina asked, miming as if she was vacuuming.

"It doesn't quite work like that," Harper said. "I don't need a lot of information. Whatever you can tell me would be appreciated, though."

"Oh, okay," Nina said, resigned.

"How long have you lived in this house?" Harper asked, pulling a small notebook out of her pocket and clicking a pen so she could take notes.

"I grew up in this house," Nina said, glancing around the immaculate farmhouse fondly. "I stayed here until I was eighteen and then I left when I got married."

"How did you end up back here?"

"I inherited the house when my mother died," Nina explained. "I thought about selling it. We had a nice house on Plum Street downtown. It was a corner lot and everything. I loved this house, though, and the idea of selling it gutted me."

Harper nodded sympathetically. She'd never formed attachments to homes, but she could see why some people did.

"I talked my husband into moving out here even though he wasn't thrilled with the idea," Nina said. "He finally relented because he thought it would be a great place to raise kids. We don't have to worry about traffic or them being grabbed off the street."

"That's good," Harper said, hoping to encourage Nina's story along.

"If we don't get rid of this ghost my husband is going to leave me," Nina said. "He's already demanding we move back to town. I don't want to give up my house."

"I'm sure we'll be able to handle the situation," Harper said. "We've done this numerous times. We need to get a feel for the spirit. When was the first time you noticed it?"

"Well, we moved into the house a year ago," Nina said, tilting her head to the side. "I guess it was our third night here when we heard noises. We chalked it up to old pipes, but it kept happening. The noises were bad, but we could mostly ignore them. It was when other things started happening that Ted – that's my husband – started making noises about moving. I've been able to put him off until now, but after yesterday … ."

"What other things started happening?"

"Things moved," Nina said. "I never saw them move at first. It started with simple things. I would put my glasses down on the end table and when I would come back they would be on the coffee table. I honestly thought I was doing it myself and forgetting, but then one day I put a book down on the couch and when I came back it was on the bookshelf."

"That's weird," Harper said. "What else?"

"One morning I came downstairs and all of my dishes were rearranged," Nina replied. "They were moved from the cupboards I had them in to the cupboards my mother used to have them in."

"Do you think this ghost knew how your mother did things?"

"Absolutely," Nina said, nodding. "I could put up with most of this but Ted, well, he's starting to freak out."

"What happened to Ted yesterday?"

"He was taking a shower and when he got out the mirror was all fogged up and … well … someone wrote a message in the fog."

"What did it say?" Harper was intrigued.

"Um … basically it told him to go on a diet." Nina looked embarrassed.

"I'm sorry?"

"It said 'lose some weight, fat ass,'" Nina said.

Harper bit the inside of her cheek to keep from laughing out loud. "Is your husband fat?"

"He's not fat," Nina said. "He has packed on a few pounds in the last year. All the ghost stuff is making him stress eat. I don't blame him."

Harper didn't either. "Who do you think the ghost is? Is it an old family member? Do you have any ideas?"

"Oh, I know exactly who it is," Nina said. "She's been leaving me messages, too. She writes them on the chalkboard in the kitchen when she's bored."

"Who is it?"

"My mother."

Harper frowned, realization washing over her. "Oh."

"I know what you're thinking," Nina said, lowering her eyes. "You think I should be grateful to still have a part of my mother left and not want to see her go."

"That's not what I was thinking."

Nina ignored Harper's statement. "I loved my mother. I did. I still do, don't get me wrong. She's just so ... harsh."

"What kind of messages is she leaving you?" Harper asked, her mind wandering to what a nightmare it would be to have her own mother haunting her. She involuntarily shuddered at the thought.

"Oh, you know, 'your dress is too low cut,' 'your children should behave better,' 'your husband is a dildo.' Basic stuff like that."

Harper swallowed the mad urge to laugh. She was starting to like this ghost. "What's your mother's name?"

"Matilda."

"Can you think of any reason she would have remained behind instead of passing over?" Harper asked.

Nina's face was blank. "What do you mean?"

"Most people want to pass over when they die," Harper explained. "The ones who stayed behind are usually jerked out of a life they weren't ready to leave. Did your mother die in a surprise accident? Was she ... murdered?"

"Oh, nothing like that," Nina said. "She had cancer. She knew she was dying for two years."

"Why did she stay?"

"She lived to nag," Nina said. "She once told me she wouldn't leave this Earth until I finally grew a brain and picked a better husband. I didn't know she was being literal when she said it. I know my mother hates Ted, but ... well ... I love him.

"He's not a perfect husband, but he is a wonderful man and great father," she continued. "No one is perfect."

"No," Harper agreed.

"I love my mother, but I'm ready to let her go," Nina said. "Just once I would like to wake up in the morning and not find my thongs in the garbage can."

"I ... what?" Harper was confused.

"She thought only prostitutes and burlesque dancers wore thongs."

"Oh," Harper said, wishing Zander had been present for this intake interview. "Well ... I'm sure we can handle this and probably pretty quickly. Do you know where your mother's spirit usually hangs out during the day?"

"In the greenhouse," Nina said. "That was her favorite place and she had a whole garden in there. She's really mad at the way I let it go so she's started cleaning it up herself. I'm sorry. I know she loved the building. I don't like dirt, though."

Harper could sympathize with that. "I'm on it. We'll get this handled today."

"Good," Nina said, exhaling heavily. "If Mom gooses Ted with invisible hands one more time he's going to have a heart attack – or a meltdown. Nobody wants that."

"THIS COULD BE the best ghost ever," Zander said, moving next to Harper in the center of the greenhouse. "She writes derogatory messages to her son-in-law. She moves dishes back to the way she likes them. She calls her grandkids brats. She's awesome."

"Imagine living with your mother's spirit after she passes on," Harper prodded.

"Oh, my mother is never going to die," Zander said. "She can't. I won't allow it."

As much as he complained about his mother and her antics Zander was dedicated to the woman who gave him life. He really would be lost without her. Harper, on the other hand, loved her mother but found it easier to do from a distance. "You're right," she said. "Your mother is going to live forever."

"Like *Fame*," Zander said, a faraway look on his face.

"I was thinking more like *Highlander*."

"I can live with that," Zander said. "I'm not thrilled with all the head chopping in that series, though."

"Movies," Harper corrected.

"The series was better," Zander argued. "The actors were hotter."

"Sean Connery is the king of hot."

"He's old."

"He's still hot," Harper argued.

"Is he as hot as the new cop?" Zander asked, shifting the conversation to a subject he was dying to talk about.

"What is your fascination with Jared Monroe?" Harper asked, irritated.

"I think you like him."

"I think I hate him," Harper said. "Did I tell you what he said to me last night?" Harper didn't give Zander a chance to respond. Instead she launched into a righteous diatribe.

"I've heard all of this," Zander said, cutting Harper off before she could get a full head of steam. "Actually, to be fair, this would've been the third time I had to listen to it. I'm not doing it again."

"He's an ass."

"He might be," Zander conceded. "He also might be a guy who has never experienced anything paranormal so he can't wrap his brain around it. That doesn't mean he's a bad guy."

"I think he is," Harper said. "He talked down to me."

"I talk down to you all of the time," Zander pointed out.

"I don't like it then either."

"You don't usually take it so personally," Zander said. "Do you want to know what I think?"

"Nope." Harper shifted her gaze from her best friend to the door of the greenhouse. "Are Molly and Eric in place?"

Zander ignored the question. "I think you like him."

"I already told you that I hate him."

"Fine, maybe you don't like him," Zander said. "I think you're attracted to him, though."

Harper snorted. "Whatever. He's not appealing to me in the slightest."

Zander didn't believe her. "Really? You don't want to see if his body is as hard as it looks under those shirts he wears? Or if his jeans really are covering up the world's best rear end? You don't like those blue eyes of his and the way they pop out against all that dark hair he has? You don't want to run your hand over that stubbled chin of his?"

"I see you've given this some thought," Harper said, nonplussed.

"He's hot."

"I don't think he plays for your team."

"He doesn't," Zander said. "Do you know how I know? Every time I'm checking him out he's checking you out – and that includes last night because I was watching you when you didn't know it."

"You were spying on me?"

"I was watching the two of you interact," Zander corrected. "I'm allowed. I'm your best friend. It's my job to make sure you're safe."

"It's your job to feed me ice cream when I have PMS."

"I do that, too."

Harper couldn't argue because he was telling the truth. "I think you're imagining things."

"I think you're pretending nothing is there when there might be a little something there," Zander countered.

"Whatever."

"We're not done talking about this," Zander warned. "For now, though, I'm going to let it go because we have a job to do."

"Great," Harper said sarcastically.

"We're going to talk about your tone, too."

"Fine," Harper said. "Do you want to get into position or are you going to imagine a few more boyfriends for me?"

"I'm not imagining it," Zander said, but he was already striding toward the east side of the structure.

"Was he really checking me out?" Harper asked.

Zander couldn't hide his smirk. "I knew you liked him."

"I don't like him," Harper said. "I find him … repugnant."

"Keep telling yourself that."

"I can guarantee that there will never be anything romantic between Jared Monroe and myself," Harper said. "We're from two different worlds. Those worlds are never going to collide."

"I'm going to remind you how wrong you were on this subject

every day for the rest of our lives when I'm proven right," Zander warned.

"Right back at you," Harper shot back.

It was a battle of wills and they both knew it. Only one of them could be right. Now the question was: Which one?

TEN

"How do I look?"

Zander pranced into the living room later that night dressed in his favorite jeans and "special occasion" black shirt. The shirt was so tight it left nothing to the imagination – which was exactly the look Zander was going for on his big date with the waiter.

"You look handsome," Harper said, glancing up from her spot on the couch where she was flipping through a magazine. "Wow. You even washed your hair."

"I had to. Matilda was a crazy ghost and even though she threw that pot at you the dirt from inside got all over me. I can't go out with my possible soul mate with dirt in my hair."

Harper smirked. "Your possible soul mate? What are you going to call him when this relationship goes south?"

"The guy who serves the crappy clam chowder," Zander replied, nonplussed. "Come on. Focus on me. Is there anything about this outfit that makes me look fat?"

Since Harper and Zander had been inseparable since kindergarten Harper's mother, Gloria, was convinced her daughter was missing out on having a female best friend. What Gloria never realized was that Zander was better than any run-of-the-mill female friend. He was the best of both worlds. He could sit on the couch and commiserate over a pint of ice cream and then obsess about the calories an hour later. What more could a girl ask for?

"You look great," Harper said, turning her attention back to the magazine.

If she thought the conversation was over with, she was sadly mistaken. "Harp, turn away from the magazine and pay attention to me."

Harper sighed and tossed the magazine onto the couch, resigned. "I'm focused on you. What should I specifically be paying attention to?"

"Do I smell like I'm expecting sex or am I merely leaving the door open for it?" Zander asked, leaning over so Harper could inhale his new cologne.

"You smell like ... ." Harper wrinkled her nose. "What is that?"

"Polo Blue."

"Is that different than regular Polo?"

"Duh."

Harper pinched Zander's side. "You smell great. You look great. Stop fussing about this. Whenever you go out with a new guy we go through this rigmarole. You're the handsomest guy in town. You know it and I know it."

"What about Jared Monroe?" Zander teased.

"Do not go there."

"We're still not done talking about him, but I don't have time for a big fight and the ice cream that will follow us making up," Zander said. "We're talking about this tomorrow, though."

"I can't wait."

"Neither can I," Zander said. He glanced down at Harper. "What are you going to do tonight?"

"I'm going to watch television and go to bed early."

Zander frowned. "Your social life is tragic when I'm not around to force you to engage with others," he said. "If I left you to your own devices you would spend your days in pajamas and curlers."

"Curlers?"

"You know what I mean," Zander said. "This is why I think Jared would be good for you."

"I thought we were waiting until tomorrow to talk about this," Harper said.

"If you were to date Jared you could be couch potatoes together," Zander said.

"What makes you think he's a couch potato?"

"He certainly doesn't look like a party person," Zander said. "In fact ... he kind of looks like he's the outdoorsy type." Zander involuntarily shuddered. "Don't worry. We can work around that. Don't ever let him talk you into going ice fishing, though. Jerry Douglas told me it was fun in high school and it was not fun."

Harper giggled, love for her best friend washing over her. "I'll keep that in mind."

"Seriously, though, I wish you wouldn't sit here alone all the time when I'm out," Zander said. "I worry about you."

"You never have to worry about me," Harper said. "I ... ." She broke off, the rest of her sentence left hanging in the ether when the sound of someone rummaging around in their kitchen assailed her ears. Since Zander and Harper were the only ones home that meant someone else had entered the house. "Who?"

Zander leaned over so he could see into the kitchen, grimacing when he shifted back to his previous spot. "You don't want to know."

"I ... ." Harper narrowed her eyes. "Who? Should I run now?"

"Where are you going to run?"

Harper recognized her mother's voice before she even walked into the living room. Zander made a comical face, raising his eyebrows and swallowing his upper lip with his lower as Harper came to grips with her mother's appearance.

As an only child, Harper liked things a certain way. She was used to solitude – and she genuinely enjoyed it. She liked spending time with Zander even though she was also perfectly happy on her own. She enjoyed spending time with her father because they were two individuals who could hang out in the same room without feeling the need to fill awkward conversational gaps. What Harper and her mother shared was completely different.

"Hello, Gloria," Zander said, forcing a smile for the visiting woman's benefit. "How are you this fine spring evening?"

"I think I have crabs," Gloria said, her blond corkscrew curls standing on end when she finally popped into Harper's field of vision.

"Mom!" Harper was mortified.

"I do," Gloria said. "I'm very itchy ... down there ... and the guy I've been seeing is a stud. I think he's gotten around a time or two."

Phil and Gloria Harlow spent twenty-eight horrible years together before they called time on their marriage and filed for divorce. When she was a teenager, Harper imagined that her parents only stayed married because of her. She was convinced they would announce their divorce the second she left for college.

It didn't happen.

After that, Harper was convinced they were waiting for her to graduate from college. The day after her graduation party she expected a phone call announcing their split.

It didn't happen.

Every year Harper came up with a scenario where they would tell her they were getting divorced.

When it didn't happen time after time, Harper lulled herself into a false sense of security. Her parents were screamers. They liked to fight. Maybe that revved their motors. That's the only way Harper could rationalize their union.

When she was finally settled and ready to embrace the fact they were going to stay together despite their mutual hatred of one another they yanked the rug out from under her and announced their impending divorce.

They were still in the process of it – even though they'd told her a year before – and the fight was getting ugly. They'd taken to arguing about who got what spoons. Harper was willing to buy them both their own set to let it go, but getting in the middle of the two of them was akin to a scene from *The Hunger Games* so Harper learned her lesson about getting involved. Well ... mostly.

Even though she was resigned to the divorce she was still grappling with watching them date. It was like the worst sitcom ever – only she was the punch line.

"I'm sure you don't have crabs," Zander said. "Does anyone still get crabs? That's such a lame STD. You probably have a yeast infection. Have you been having a lot of sex? I've read that if you have a lot of sex it can lead to a yeast infection."

Harper was horrified. "Where on Earth did you read that?"

"We have a subscription to Cosmopolitan," Zander reminded her.

"*You* have a subscription," Harper corrected.

"You read the sex articles, too," Zander said. "Don't even deny it."

"Why would Harper read the sex articles?" Gloria asked. "Don't you have to engage in sex to read about it? I think that should be the rule."

"Thank you, Mother," Harper said, shooting Gloria a death glare. "Why are you here?"

"I need a slutty skirt," Gloria said. "I have a date tonight and I need something that shows off my legs and gives Walter easy access if he wants it."

Harper seriously thought she was going to throw up. "I don't have a slutty skirt."

"You're dating a man named Walter?" Zander asked. "That's not a very sexy name." Even though Gloria and Zander fought like cats and dogs they had a grudging respect for one another.

"Walter Shanks," Gloria clarified. "It's not a great name, but the things he does in bed … wowza … he can shank me whenever he wants."

Harper rolled her eyes. "I don't think that means what you think it means. Shanking is something prison inmates do to each other."

"We do that, too," Gloria said.

"Omigod." Harper covered her face with her hands. "Never tell me anything like that again. Never!"

"You don't have a problem listening to Zander talk about it," Gloria complained.

"Zander doesn't talk about things like that," Harper argued.

Gloria glanced at Zander for confirmation.

"I don't," Zander said. "Sometimes I draw her little pictures on napkins, but we don't really talk about it."

"I thought you were best friends," Gloria said. "Don't best friends talk about things like that?"

"Harper doesn't have a frame of reference and she freaks out at sex talk," Zander explained. "I can't explain it. I think she might be frigid."

"I am not frigid!"

"Oh, chill out," Gloria said, rolling her eyes. "I need a skirt."

"I don't have a slutty skirt," Harper said. "I already told you that."

"I think you're making that up," Gloria challenged.

"Go and look in my closet," Harper said, pinching the bridge of her nose to ward off the raging headache she was sure was only seconds away from descending. "Take whatever you want."

Gloria brightened. "Thank you."

She disappeared down the hallway and Harper waited until she was sure her mother was out of earshot before she turned on Zander. "You did that on purpose," she hissed. "You know I don't like it when you encourage the sex talk from her."

"Your mother is going through an … awakening," Zander said. "I think you should support her instead of making faces every time she shows up for guidance and help."

"You know she calls you 'the big poof' when you're not around, right?" Harper asked.

"Fine. Set her on fire."

Harper scorched Zander with a look. "That's not helping. I don't want to deal with this. I'm too old to deal with this. I don't want to hear about how much sex she's having with Walter."

"Walter Shanks is a really crappy name," Zander mused. "I wonder what he does for a living."

"He's a lawyer," Gloria said, breezing back into the room with a black skirt draped over her arm.

Harper's cheeks burned. Was her mother eavesdropping? Had she heard everything they'd said?

"What did you find?" Zander asked, unruffled by the possibility of being caught talking badly about Gloria.

Gloria held up the simple black skirt. "It's the only thing she had that made me think I wouldn't want to kill myself if I was forced to wear it."

"It's not very sexy," Zander said.

"It will be when I get done putting a slit in it," Gloria said, moving toward the front door. "I'll bring it back when I'm done."

"Keep it," Harper said, waving her mother off. "I'm not going to want it after you finish ... whoring it up."

"Way to stay positive, Harper," Gloria deadpanned. "Zander, have a good evening with your date ... and I only call you a poof on special occasions."

"That's good to know," Zander said, dropping a kiss on Gloria's cheek. "I'll walk you out. I'm leaving anyway."

"Oh, that's nice," Gloria said.

Zander shot one more look in Harper's direction. "Try to do something fun while I'm gone. Going to bed early and reading a book doesn't count."

"I'll keep that in mind," Harper said, her tone dry.

Once the door was shut and the house was empty of everything but Harper's busy mind, the intrepid blonde ghost hunter waited exactly five minutes before she flipped the magazine shut and got to her feet.

She'd been lying when she told Zander she had nothing planned. She had something planned ... it was just something he wasn't going to like. After a few hours of searching on the Internet during the afternoon stretch, Harper found an address for Annie Dresden. Zander mentioned it before but she didn't want to bring it up and tip him off regarding what she had planned. She was going to visit the woman's house in search of a lost soul. She didn't want to tell Zander because he was likely to cancel his date to watch her. She didn't want that.

Once Harper was sure Zander wasn't returning, she grabbed her keys off the table by the front door and hopped out of the house. She thought briefly about changing from her comfortable pink sleep pants and tank top but decided better of it, instead grabbing a hoodie to cover her should she get cold.

It's not like she was going to see anyone she cared about. After all, she didn't care what anyone thought about her clothes anyway.

She wasn't prepared for just how wrong that way of thinking was about to go.

ELEVEN

Annie Dresden's rental property was something of an enigma. After spending twenty minutes watching the small ranch house from her purple Ford Focus trying to decide the best way to search the property, Harper approached it cautiously. In truth, she really wanted to make sure no one was inside the house.

It was dark and empty. The occupant was never coming home – not as a living entity, at least.

Harper didn't know what she expected. The property appeared close to the St. Clair Community College campus on a map, but it was actually surrounded by woods. Since it was dark, Harper couldn't ascertain if there was a trail that led through the thick trees. She guessed it didn't matter. Still, the quiet house was not how Harper remembered her college days.

Even though the house was isolated Harper knew her plaid, cotton sleep pants stood out against the stark night sky. They were pink and white, and the tank top she was wearing was also pink – although she'd opted for a black hoodie to wear over it. If anyone was watching there was no way she could hide. She silently cursed herself for not taking the time to change her clothes, but it was too late now. She was here and she had a task to do.

Harper pocketed her keys and took an arcing trek around the house. She was used to ghosts, but she wasn't above a good scare from time to time. Since she was alone, she didn't want to panic if Annie Dresden popped up out of nowhere.

As she stepped to the side of the house Harper moved close enough to peer through a window. The moon was bright, but it didn't give off enough illumination to give Harper an idea of how Annie lived and that was something Harper realized she needed to know if she was going to discover how the woman died.

"Are you a pervert or something?"

Harper jumped when she heard the voice, pasting a rueful smile on her face as she turned and regarded Annie's ethereal visage. "Not last time I checked," she said. "My best friend told me I was frigid before he left on his date tonight."

Annie arched an eyebrow, a mannerism remaining from life. There was a sardonic twist about it Harper couldn't help but enjoy. "You're best friends with a man?" Annie asked. "How does that work?"

"We've been best friends since elementary school so I've never really known friendship to be any other way," Harper explained.

"How come you don't date? If you like each other so much you would think dating would be the logical next step."

"He's gay."

"Ah."

"And kind of fickle," Harper added. "He's the best friend I've ever had and he will always be a sort of ... soul mate ... for me. We could never be in a relationship, though. Even if he wasn't gay that would never work out."

"Is he ugly?" Annie asked, genuinely curious.

"No. He's just a constant pain in my rear end," Harper said. "If we dated I'd have to smother him in his sleep. His antics are a lot funnier when romantic love isn't attached to them."

Annie laughed, the sound full of mirth despite her circumstances. "You're funny. Is he funny, too?"

"He's very funny," Harper said. "You'd probably like him."

"Is he the guy who was at the beach with you today?"

"That's him," Harper said, hoping that holding up her end of a friendly conversation would be enough to get Annie to trust her. She was determined to help, but she needed information to do it. Annie wasn't going to trust a stranger with the biggest secrets of her life ... even if they led to eventually solving her death. "He keeps making me go to the same café on Main Street because he's been cruising the waiter. He finally went out with him tonight so we can start eating at more than one restaurant."

"Wouldn't he want to see his new boyfriend more often?"

"He'll only date him a few times before he finds something tragically wrong with him and has to dump him," Harper replied.

Annie smiled, the expression lighting up her pallid features. "He sounds wonderful."

"He is," Harper said, sympathy tugging at her heart.

"He obviously knows you can ... do this," Annie said, gesturing widely.

"Talk to ghosts? Yes."

"Ghosts," Annie said, rolling the word around as she tried to digest it. "I know that's what I am, but I'm having a hard time ... understanding ... how it happened."

"What do you remember?" Harper asked.

"I ... it's a blur," Annie said. "I remember being on campus. I met a few people for coffee at the university center. Everyone has been really stressed out because of finals."

"I remember that time of year," Harper said. "What happened next?"

"They were all going to the bar and they wanted me to come, but I decided to be responsible," Annie said, snorting as she realized what she was saying. "Being responsible led to my death. That is just so ..."

"Disappointing?" Harper supplied.

"Bleeding tragic," Annie said. "My mother always told me I was too serious. It's hard to believe, but if I had been less responsible and blown off a night of studying at the library I probably would still be alive."

"You can't go back and change it," Harper said. "We can only move forward."

"What's forward?" Annie asked. "My life is over. I have nothing left to move forward to."

"That is not true," Harper said. "There's another place out there. I've seen it. Granted, I've only gotten glimpses in flashes when I send spirits through to the other side, but every time I go there I feel the warmth and happiness associated with it."

"I don't understand," Annie said, although her interest was piqued. "Are you talking about Heaven?"

Harper balked at the distinction. She'd never given a word to the "other place" because she was afraid if she did she would have to acknowledge the probability that a third place existed for ... darker spirits. Only once did she think she caught sight of it – craggy, cold rocks and ominous shadows filling her heart with dread – and she'd quickly opted to push it out of her mind. She only wanted to believe in the good place.

"If that's what you believe," Harper said. "This isn't the end for you. This is simply a ... layover."

"A layover for what?"

"I think you're still here because you want someone to pay for killing you," Harper explained.

"Do you know how I died?" Annie asked. "I keep trying to remember, but it's ... it's like trying to remember things you did when you were really drunk. The memories feel like they should be there, but they aren't."

"Don't push yourself," Harper said. "If you're having trouble remembering it's because it was traumatic for you. When you're ready to remember, you will."

"What should I do until then?" Annie asked. "Are you going to help me cross over now?"

Harper bit her lip, unsure how to proceed. She wanted to put Annie to rest, but she still needed her help to solve a murder. She was hoping Annie would understand that. "If you want to cross over now I can help you," she hedged. "It's just ... I was hoping you would be willing to hang around until we know who killed you."

"Of course," Annie said. "That's the way it should be. I didn't think of that. I've been so ... lost. My mother was here earlier today. She looks like she's aged ten years. I'm scared that my death is going to kill her, too."

"You can't worry about that," Harper said. "We can only do what we can do. I've learned that the hard way on more than one occasion. You can't help everyone, but you can help those who want to be helped. I'm guessing you want to be helped. Am I right?"

"I do," Annie said. "Where do we start?"

"Go back to when you were at the library," Harper prodded. "Do you remember seeing anyone you recognized?"

Annie screwed up her face in concentration, tilting her head to the side as she considered the question. "Not really," she said. "The library wasn't exactly a hub even when the end of the year wasn't looming. There weren't a lot of people there and that's why I wanted to go there. I knew it would be private."

"Did you live here alone?"

Annie nodded. "My mother worried about me being on my own so she constantly stopped by, though. I didn't want to risk it when I had so much to do. That's why I went to the library. I guess that was another fatal miscalculation."

"Annie, you have to remember that the worst has already happened to you," Harper said, her voice low and soothing. "You can't die a second time."

"Are you saying I've already survived dying?" Annie asked, chuckling hoarsely.

"In a way," Harper said, joining in with the laughter. "Do you remember leaving the library?"

"I remember packing up my stuff."

"Your stuff? Did you have a bag?"

"Yes," Annie said. "I had an economics textbook, my wallet, a couple of notebooks, and my iPad inside of it."

"You weren't found with any of that stuff," Harper mused.

"I wasn't found with my clothing either," Annie griped. "Do you think … ?" She broke off, the question too horrible to ask.

"I don't know," Harper said. "I hope not, but … . I think they're getting your autopsy results back tomorrow. Go back to the library, though. Would you have left out of a specific door?"

"I always park on the east side of the library," Annie said.

"What kind of car?"

"It's a 2005 red Ford Explorer," Annie said. "It wasn't much to look at, but it was dependable."

"Do you remember getting in the Explorer?"

"No."

Harper rubbed the spot between her eyebrows. "Do you think you made it back here?"

"I honestly don't remember," Annie said.

Harper was starting to get frustrated. The holes in Annie's memory were definitely a hindrance. "Do you remember anyone talking to you after you separated from your friends?"

"I just remember sitting at the table in the library," Annie said.

Harper blew out a frustrated sigh. "Well … I guess that's all we can do tonight."

"There's an easy way of knowing if I ever made it back here," Annie suggested.

Harper glanced up, hopeful.

"I always put my book bag on the table in the kitchen because I go in through the back door when I come home," Annie said. "If my bag is there that means I came back here. I don't know if that helps, but it's something."

"Except I can't go in your house," Harper said.

"Why not?"

"It's called breaking and entering. I would go to jail."

"I'm giving you permission," Annie said.

"That's nice, but I'm not sure it will stand up in court," Harper replied.

"No one is out here," Anne said, glancing around to make sure she was telling the truth. You don't have to search the house. You only have to open the back door and see if my bag is on the table. That would at least tell us if I disappeared between the library and here. I wasn't stopping anywhere else."

Harper sighed, hating that Annie was making sense even though she knew it was a bad idea. "I have no way of getting in," Harper said, almost relieved at the realization. "I'm not kicking the door in."

"There's a spare key hidden under the turtle planter on the back porch," Annie said.

Of course there was. Harper sighed, resigned. "I guess that means I should probably look at the table."

"It won't take long," Annie said, moving along the side of the house and gesturing for Harper to follow. "I need to know if I made it home. I have no idea why it's important to me, but it is."

"You want to know if you were ... violated ... here," Harper said. "You probably have fond memories of this place and don't want them tainted."

"I did love this house," Annie mused. "Mom wanted me to live closer to campus, but I fell in love with this house."

Harper stepped up onto the back patio and peered into the gloom. "Where is the planter?"

"Over here."

Harper followed the sound of Annie's voice. She almost tripped over the turtle before she found it. She pulled the arms of her hoodie down to cover her hands and then lifted the turtle up to find a gleaming key right where Annie indicated it would be.

"What are you doing with the sleeves of your hoodie?" Annie asked.

"In case they check for fingerprints I don't want to have to explain mine here," Harper said, carefully grasping the key through the fabric.

"I guess you've done this before," Annie said.

"It's not my first time," Harper agreed. She slipped the key into the lock, the sound of it tumbling to signify the door was opening filling her with a mixture of dread and relief. "I'm just looking really quickly to see if the bag is here. I'm not doing anything else."

"That's good."

The voice coming out of the blackness caused Harper's heart to skip a beat. It belonged to a man, and for a moment she wondered if a murderer was about to claim another victim. When a small flashlight snapped on and landed on her face she was momentarily blinded. That's when she recognized the voice.

"I can't wait to hear how you're going to explain this," Jared said.

"Uh-oh," Annie muttered.

"Yeah," Harper said, exhaling sharply. "Uh-oh."

TWELVE

"It's a nice evening for a walk," Harper said, fidgeting nervously. "That's what I was doing, by the way."

"With a key to a murder victim's house?" Jared pressed.

"I ... can you not shine that light in my eyes? It hurts." Harper was irritated. She couldn't decide if being caught or standing so close to Jared was the primary cause of her agitation.

Jared lowered the light and it took a few seconds for Harper's eyes to adjust. When they did, she found Jared watching her with a mixture of curiosity and annoyance. "What are you doing here?"

"I was taking a walk."

"And you decided to let yourself into Annie Dresden's house?"

"I ... ."

"He's really handsome," Annie said.

"He's still an idiot," Harper muttered.

Jared glanced around. He couldn't figure out whom Harper was talking to. "Are you talking to someone on one of those ear things? Mel says you and Zander use them on your ghost busting cases. Is that who you're talking to?"

"I ... ." That would be a feasible excuse except Harper didn't have an earbud with her. "I was talking to myself."

"I see," Jared said, choosing his words carefully. "So you were calling me an idiot while carrying on a conversation with yourself?"

"Yes."

"I know this is really bad for you, but he is so hot," Annie said.

A biting retort was on the tip of Harper's tongue, but she opted not to release it. She had no idea how she was going to get out of this situation but unleashing a bevy of insults and hurling them in Jared's direction didn't seem like the smart way to go.

"Ms. Harlow, I need to know what you're doing here," Jared said, changing his tactics. "I also wouldn't mind knowing why you're out walking in your pajamas. I love the pink, by the way."

"Those pants are really cute," Annie said.

Harper pinched the bridge of her nose. She was caught. She knew it and she was pretty sure Jared knew it, too. There was no way out of this situation. The only thing she had was truth – and it was going to make Jared think she was even crazier than he already did. "Fine," she gritted out. "I came here because I wanted to see if I could find Annie's ghost. I wanted to know if she remembered anything about her death."

Jared pursed his lips and nodded. "I see. Did you find her ghost?"

Harper glanced at Annie. "Yes."

"Did she tell you how she died?"

"She doesn't remember how she died," Harper said. "She remembers getting coffee with friends and going to the library. Everything after that is a blank."

"The ghost has memory gaps?" Jared was amused.

"It's very traumatic for spirits when they first come to grips with their new reality."

"You can say that again," Annie said.

"And why were you breaking into Annie's house?"

"I wasn't technically breaking in," Harper said. "Annie gave me her permission. She wanted me to see if her book bag was on the table on the other side of the door because that would mean she made it home."

Jared furrowed his brow. "There's no bag on that table."

"There's not?" Harper didn't know if that was good news or bad news.

Jared shook his head. "We were here earlier. There's no bag on the table."

"He's right," Annie said, glancing into the kitchen. "I guess I should have remembered that. I was inside with my mom earlier. I was more focused on her, though."

"We also should've remembered that you can walk through walls and I didn't need to use a key to look inside," Harper grumbled. "I knew that was a stupid move."

"Oh, yeah, I never thought of that," Annie said. "I'm sorry. I'm still getting used to all of this."

"It's not your fault."

Jared made a face. "Are you talking to Annie right now?"

"I'm not crazy," Harper snapped.

"I didn't say you were crazy. I asked if you were talking to Annie."

"Yes."

"Okay," Jared said. "Well, I think we need to have a little talk down at the station."

"What?" Harper's heart flopped. "I ... you're arresting me?"

"I'm taking you in for questioning," Jared stressed.

"But ... my car is here."

"Is that the purple one in the driveway?"

"Yes. Is that how you knew I was here?" Harper narrowed her eyes. "Were you following me?"

"Don't flatter yourself," Jared said. "I was checking out the house because I wanted to make sure no one stopped by to ... break in ... or anything. "This is not technically my jurisdiction, although the St. Clair Police Department gave us permission to come and go from the property as we please."

"Wait a second," Harper said, realization dawning. "This isn't your jurisdiction. That means you can't arrest me. You don't have the authority."

"That's not exactly true," Jared said. "I ... ."

"You can't tell me what to do," Harper said, her tone haughty. "You don't have the power."

"Ms. Harlow ...."

"I'm leaving," Harper said, moving away from the door. "I'm sorry to have ruined your night with ghost stories. It won't happen again. I can promise you that."

"Ms. Harlow ...."

"Have a nice night," Harper said, smiling at Jared and turning to walk off the back porch. Jared's hand shot out, grabbing her arm at the elbow and stilling her.

"Ms. Harlow, I can assure you that you're wrong about my powers in this situation," Jared said. "I witnessed you breaking the law. I have no choice but to take you in."

"Are you seriously telling me you're arresting me?" Harper was incensed. "You can't be serious."

"Oh, I'm serious," Jared said.

"You're going to regret this!"

"WHERE IS SHE?" Zander stormed into the Whisper Cove Police Department and scanned the small front lobby for his uncle.

Mel ran his tongue over his teeth, cringing at the fury on his nephew's face, and then leaned forward so he could meet Zander's angry gaze. "Now, Zander ...."

"Where is she?" Zander repeated. "How could you arrest her?"

"I didn't arrest her," Mel said. "In fact, I wasn't even there. My partner arrested her."

"Officer Going-To-Be-Single-Forever? Where is he?"

Mel stilled, surprised by Zander's vehemence. "What is that supposed to mean?"

"It means I kind of liked him and thought he was interested in Harper before ... this," Zander snapped. "Where is she? I want to see her right now."

"Jared is in the back questioning her," Mel said. "How did you even know she was here?"

"Amy Dandridge saw her being led into the back of the station in cuffs," Zander said. "She called my mother."

"Your mother knows?" Mel didn't look thrilled with the prospect. "Can I assume she'll be calling soon?"

"She got me on my cell phone while I was on a date," Zander said.

"I'm sorry your date got interrupted."

"I'm not. He talked with his mouth full of food. It was never going to work out."

Mel sighed. "When is your mother calling?"

"She had one more call to make before she had a glass of bourbon and called you," Zander said, smiling evilly at his uncle.

"I'm almost afraid to ask," Mel muttered. "Who did she call?"

Zander didn't need to answer because Gloria Harlow picked that moment to roll into the office with her own date hot on her heels. "Where is my daughter?"

"Oh, no," Mel said, his mouth dropping open. "This is not good."

"You should've thought about that before you arrested my daughter, Melvin Egbert Kelsey," Gloria yelled.

Mel's face drained of color. Since he'd gone to school with Gloria she knew all of his secrets – even the ones he hoped were buried forever. "Now, Gloria ...."

"Don't you 'now Gloria' me," Gloria ordered. "I want to know why my daughter has been arrested."

"She was caught breaking and entering at a murder victim's home," Jared said, appearing from the back hallway and scanning the new faces in the room. "Who are you?"

"Who am I?" Gloria was beside herself. "I'm the landscaper and you're the ass grass man I'm about to mow."

"I think you got that saying wrong," Zander offered.

"Shut up, Zander," Gloria snapped.

"Who is she?" Jared asked, turning his attention to Mel.

"This is Gloria Harlow," Mel said, his voice shaky. "She's Harper's mother."

"That's right," Gloria said. "I'm her mother ... and you have no idea how ticked off I am."

"Am I supposed to be frightened about that?"

"You're supposed to realize that I'm going to … mow your ass," Gloria said, miming some activity that looked more like pushing a shopping cart than anything else.

"Why did you arrest Harper?" Zander asked, turning to Jared.

"She was breaking into Annie Dresden's house."

"That's not your jurisdiction," Zander pointed out. "You don't have the authority to arrest her."

"I have the authority to arrest anyone breaking the law," Jared countered. "She was breaking the law. I don't care what she says – or what tall tales she comes up with to excuse it – but those are the hard facts. I saw her get the key from under a pot and open the door."

"That's not breaking and entering," Zander said. "She had a key."

"To a dead woman's house."

"She probably had permission to enter," Zander sniffed, crossing his arms over his chest. "You can't arrest her if she has permission."

"And who gave her this permission?" Jared asked. "The dead woman? If you're going to tell me that I'm going to arrest you for lying to a police officer."

"Wait just a minute," Mel said, holding his hand up. "You can't arrest Zander. He's only here because he's worried about Harper."

"Go ahead and arrest me," Zander hissed. "I can't wait until that little tidbit gets around town. You'll be fired faster than Julia Nixon's panties get tossed every Friday night."

Now Jared was the one who was confused. "Who is Julia Nixon?"

"She's the town … ." Mel broke off, searching for a kind word to use.

"Tramp," Gloria supplied.

"I was going to say bike," Zander said.

"Bike?" Jared arched an eyebrow.

"Everyone gets a ride," Zander said, making a face. "Please don't tell me you've never heard that joke."

"Not used to refer to a … woman," Jared said.

"I'm not going to stand for this," Gloria said. "I want my daughter released right now."

"I'm not done questioning her," Jared replied, refusing to back down even though he felt woefully outnumbered.

"What are you even asking her?" Zander asked.

"I want to know how she knew where to find that key and how she knew how to look for the book bag Annie was carrying the night she died," Jared said. "Until she gives me satisfactory answers she's staying here."

"Annie told her," Zander said.

"Annie is dead."

"And Harper talks to ghosts," Gloria said. "Oh, don't bother looking at me that way, Melvin. I know you don't believe it. Heck, I didn't believe it the first few times she did it. It's true, though. She only went to that house because she wants to help Annie."

"She should've waited for me," Zander grumbled. "I could've served as lookout so this didn't happen. I wonder why she didn't tell me she was going."

"Because she knew you would cancel your date to watch her instead," Gloria said. "How was your date, by the way?"

"He talked with his mouth full of food."

"Oh, well, better luck next time." Gloria patted Zander's arm for a moment and then turned back to Jared. "Let my daughter out now or I'll make you pay."

"Ma'am, I have no reason to hold your daughter – other than the fact that I think she needs mental help – as long as she tells me how she found out that information," Jared said. "I don't want to keep her here."

"The girl's ghost told her where to find that information," Gloria said. "She's not lying to you."

"I don't believe in ghosts, ma'am." Jared was firm.

"I don't care what you believe in," Gloria said. "I care about my daughter and she's not spending one more minute in this ... rat hole." Gloria snapped her fingers in the direction of her date. "This is Walter Shanks and he's an attorney. Walter, go get them."

Walter's already pale face drained of color. "What?"

"You're a lawyer," Gloria said. "Get my daughter out of here."

"I'm a tax lawyer," Walter said. "I can only help her if she's hiding funds from the IRS."

"Why is this happening?" Gloria screeched.

JARED LET himself into the small interrogation room after a few more minutes of small town theater in the lobby. He was quiet when he opened the door, and Harper obviously didn't hear his return.

"That's something, but I'm not sure what I can do about it now," Harper said.

"What's something?" Jared asked.

Harper jumped, swiveling quickly and meeting Jared's eyes. He didn't miss the redness surrounding her blue orbs and realized she'd been crying in his absence. His heart rolled at the thought, although he couldn't figure out why.

"Nothing," Harper muttered, lowering her head to her arms.

"Have you been crying?"

"My eyes are just tired," Harper said. "It's past my bedtime."

Jared glanced at the wall clock. It was barely eleven. "You have some visitors in the lobby," he said.

"Zander?"

"And your mother," Jared said, smirking when he saw Harper's shoulders stiffen. "She's ... fun."

"Did she bring her date with her?" Harper asked, resigned.

"Yes, and she was very upset to find out he's a tax lawyer instead of a real lawyer," Jared said. "They're out there fighting about it right now."

"Oh, well, good," Harper said. "Once I'm done serving hard time I'll never hear the end of that. I guess I'm getting a double dose of cruel and unusual punishment."

Jared grinned despite the surreal situation. For a mentally unbalanced woman, she had a funny sense of humor. "Are you sticking to your ghost story?"

"It's the only story I have."

Jared exhaled heavily. "Okay. You can go."

Harper stilled. "What?"

"You can go," Jared said. "If I try to keep you here any longer I'm going to create an ... incident ... according to Mel. He's terrified of your mother, by the way."

"My mother is terrifying to everyone ... including me," Harper replied.

"She seems worried about you," Jared said. "She also believes all of this ghost business."

Harper pushed her chair back and turned so she could face Jared. "I know you think I'm crazy."

"I think that's a strong word," Jared said. "I think your belief system is ... different. I'm not saying you're crazy."

"You're not saying it because you're worried I'll sue you," Harper said. "Don't worry. I'm not litigious."

"In that case you might be crazy." Jared was going for levity and even though Harper shot him a weak smile the expression didn't make it all the way up to her eyes. "Zander will give you a ride home. You can pick your car up tomorrow morning. We had it towed here."

"Great," Harper said, glancing around the room. "Where is my purse?"

"Up at the front desk." Jared cleared out of the way so Harper could move past him. She was almost out the door before she turned back.

"I know you're not going to believe me and that's your right," Harper said. "If you're looking for Annie's car, though, the last place she saw it was on the east side of the library. She was telling me right before you came back that she remembers someone coming up behind her in the parking lot. She thinks she dropped her keys underneath the car."

Jared shifted, surprised by Harper's words. "I ... okay."

"Have a nice night," Harper said, pulling the door open and stepping into the hallway.

Jared watched her go with conflicted eyes. "Sleep well," he murmured to her back.

THIRTEEN

Harper woke up hoping the previous evening was nothing more than a bad dream. She rolled to her side, stretched, and then frowned when her eyes landed on the hoodie draped across the back of her vanity chair. It definitely wasn't a dream.

She climbed out of bed, resigned, and after a quick trip to the bathroom to splash water on her face and brush her teeth Harper found Zander standing over the stove in the kitchen with a spatula in his hand. "Hello, Jailbird," he teased.

Harper didn't bother mustering a smile. "Hello, Butthead."

Zander's face softened. "Are you okay? You were really quiet when we left the station last night. You didn't want to talk then and I let it go, but I think we should talk now."

"What is there to talk about?" Harper asked, sliding into one of the chairs around their round kitchen table and reaching for the carafe of juice so she could pour herself a glass. "What are you cooking, by the way? That smells amazing."

"I'm making omelets," Zander said. "I ran out to the market while you were still sleeping and picked up fresh eggs, mushrooms, cheese, onions, and tomatoes."

"We really need to shop more," Harper lamented.

"I think we do okay," Zander said, arching an eyebrow as he kept one eye on the omelet pan and the other on his best friend. "Tell me what happened last night."

Harper reluctantly launched into the tale, knowing full well that Zander wasn't going to let it go until he got the full story out of her. When she was done, Zander let loose with a low whistle and fixed her with a serious look. "That's a lot of information," he said. "Well, we'll start with Annie. I'm glad she finally talked to you and I'm relieved she's not traumatized. If she can help with this investigation we should be able to help her move on that much quicker."

"I feel bad for her," Harper said. "She thinks she would still be alive if she wasn't such a rule follower. She wishes she'd been more of a rebel when she still had the chance."

"Do you wish you were more of a rebel?" Zander asked sagely.

"I am a rebel," Harper scoffed. "I talk to ghosts."

"That doesn't make you a rebel," Zander argued. "That makes you talented."

"I don't think Jared Monroe sees it as a talent."

Ah, there it is, Zander internally mused. It wasn't Annie's problems plaguing Harper – well, at least not entirely. It was Jared Monroe. Zander knew something was going on there even if neither party wanted to admit it. "Harper, we both know that it takes people some time to come to grips with what you can do. He doesn't understand that what you see is real. He will eventually realize that you're as talented as you are beautiful."

Harper ran a hand through her morning-tousled hair. "I don't think he's ever going to see me as talented and he certainly doesn't see me as beautiful. He thought the pajamas I wore to Annie's house last night were cute, though."

"Those things are a travesty," Zander shot back. "They make you look fifty."

"Maybe I feel fifty."

"Maybe you're feeling sorry for yourself this morning and you should let it go," Zander suggested. "There's no reason to be all … morose."

"I'm not being morose."

"You're pouting," Zander said. "That's the same thing as being morose. This is like when you were fourteen and realized not every guy was going to be as handsome and charming as I was and there were going to be a lot of fish in the sea you were going to have to throw back."

"You always take the long way around everything," Harper complained. "We both know Jimmy Durand dumped me for Natalie Archer because she had bigger boobs. I wasn't pouting. I was resigned to my fate."

"You stuffed for a month," Zander replied. "It looked like you had lumpy socks in your bra."

"I *did* have lumpy socks in my bra."

"That's why it looked like you did," Zander said, flipping the omelet. "You're not fourteen. You don't have to stuff. You filled out naturally. I know you're feeling sorry for yourself right now, but there's no reason for it. You're a beautiful woman … even if you don't want to admit it right now."

"Why are we even talking about this?"

"Because you think Jared Monroe looks at you and sees a crazy woman who runs around in her pajamas talking to ghosts," Zander replied, not missing a beat.

"That *is* what he sees."

"He sees more than that," Zander said. "I'm curious why you care what he thinks, though. You said you weren't interested in him."

"I'm not," Harper scoffed.

"I think you might be," Zander said. "That's neither here nor there until he gets his head out of his rear end, though. For now he's off limits because he doesn't understand about the outer limits."

"Nice play on words," Harper muttered.

"Harp, I love you more than anything in this world," Zander said. "We can only handle one catastrophe at a time, though. For now, I think we should focus on Annie. The Jared stuff will work itself out when the time is right."

"How many times do I have to tell you I'm not interested in Jared Monroe?"

"Just until I believe it," Zander said, scooping the omelet onto a plate and using the spatula to cut it in half so he could divvy it up between them. "I ... ." He didn't get a chance to finish what he was about to say because the back door opened at that precise moment and Phil Harlow let himself into the kitchen. He didn't look happy.

"Hi, Dad," Harper said.

"I don't even know why we pretend to lock the doors in this house," Zander said. "Everyone just lets themselves in whenever they feel like it."

Phil grabbed one of the plates before Zander could stop him. "This looks good."

Zander sighed and shoved the second plate toward Harper before returning to the stove so he could cook another omelet for himself. "Help yourself, Phil."

"Thanks, Zander," Phil said, either missing the sarcasm or opting not to acknowledge it. He sat down in the open chair next to Harper and dug into his omelet. After tasting a sample of Zander's culinary genius, he poured himself a glass of juice and then fixed his full attention on his daughter. "I'm totally pissed off at you."

"Oh, good," Harper deadpanned. "I thought this morning couldn't get any worse. I was wrong. What did I do to you?"

"You got arrested last night and didn't bother calling your only father," Phil said. "Do you have any idea how that made me feel?"

"I didn't call anyone," Harper said. "I didn't get the chance."

"You called your mother," Phil challenged. "Sandy Hannigan said Gloria and her new boy toy showed up to bail you out."

"I wasn't charged with anything so I didn't have to be bailed out."

"I wouldn't call Walter a 'boy toy' either," Zander said. "He's more like ... a building block. One of those ones that's a knock-off, though. He's not a name brand block."

Phil snorted, winking his appreciation in Zander's direction. "Did Harper call you when she got arrested, too? Why am I always the last one to know?"

"I told you I didn't call anyone," Harper said.

"She's telling the truth," Zander offered. "My mother called me because someone saw Harper being led into the police station. After my mother was done giving me an earful she called Gloria. Harper didn't call anyone."

"Oh," Phil said, brightening considerably. "Well, that makes me feel a little bit better."

"Why?" Harper asked.

"I don't like being the forgotten parent," Phil replied. "I know it's normal for children to take sides in a divorce, but I never thought you'd take your mother's side."

"First off, I'm not taking anyone's side," Harper said. "Second ... I would never take her side even if I was taking sides."

Phil reached over and tousled Harper's already snarled hair. "That's my girl."

Zander exchanged an amused look with Harper and then turned his full attention to the new omelet. "So, Phil, I heard you're threatening to beat Gloria's new boyfriend up."

"Who told you that?" Phil asked, narrowing his blue eyes.

"Someone down at the basketball court said you were, and I quote, threatening to put a boot in Walter's ass for stealing your woman," Zander said. "I thought you wanted the divorce."

"I do want the divorce."

"Why are you calling Mom 'your woman' then?" Harper asked.

"Because we're not divorced yet and I don't like anyone taking what's mine before I'm ready to give it up," Phil said. "That's not the way things work."

"You and Mom have been haggling over everything – including thumbtacks – since you announced you were getting divorced," Harper said. "I'm starting to think it's not going to happen."

"It's happening," Phil countered. "I can't wait to get rid of that woman."

"If you say so," Harper said, finishing off her omelet and downing the rest of her glass of orange juice. "I'll hop in the shower first," she said. "We're going to have to drive together to work until I can pick up my car."

"We'll stop and get it before we go to the office," Zander said.

Harper dropped a kiss on her father's forehead as she moved past him. "It was nice seeing you, Dad. You know you can drop in for other reasons than accusing me of favoring Mom over you, right?"

"That's not what I was doing," Phil protested.

"Well, it was nice seeing you anyway." Harper shuffled down the hallway.

Phil waited until she was out of earshot before turning to Zander. "What's going on? Why is she so depressed?"

"She has a crush on the cop who arrested her," Zander said. "She's convinced that he thinks she's crazy because of the whole ghost thing."

"This is the new cop?"

Zander nodded.

"Do you like him?"

"I can't decide," Zander said. "On one hand I think he's smoking hot and he's the first guy Harper has even looked sideways at in almost two years."

"What about the other hand?" Phil pressed.

"On the other hand I'm going to have to kill him if he hurts her and that's a possibility as long as he keeps acting all weird about the ghost stuff," Zander said. "He looks like he works out. Killing him might be difficult."

Phil pursed his lips. When his daughter first started hanging out with Zander he thought it was odd for children of the opposite sex to be so close to one another. When he realized Zander was gay, he was initially uncomfortable around the teenage boy. Now he couldn't be happier that his only child had such a loyal friend. "I'll help you kill him if it comes to it."

Zander smiled. "Give it time. I think Jared just needs to wrap his mind around what's going on."

"What if he never believes?" Phil asked. "Some people are like that, you know? No matter how much proof you show them they can't accept what's happening right in front of them."

"We'll see how things go today," Zander said. "Harper gave Jared a tip on where to find the dead woman's car before leaving last night. If it pans out, I think we're going to be seeing a lot more of Jared Monroe than Harper realizes."

"How do you know she likes him?" Phil asked.

"Because she can't stop watching him when he's around," Zander replied. "I'm not saying she likes him yet. I'm definitely saying there's some sexual attraction there, though. It's mutual. Jared looks at her the same way."

"I don't know how to feel about that," Phil said. "She's my daughter. I like to think of her as sexless."

"That's funny because Harper has been doing that for two years," Zander said. "I know you're her father and you don't want to dwell on it, but she deserves some happiness."

"And you think this Jared Monroe guy could give it to her?" Phil looked both concerned and hopeful.

"I think he's our best shot right now," Zander said. "It's too early to tell, though. We'll just have to wait and see."

FOURTEEN

Jared's mood wasn't much better than Harper's when he rolled into the station. Mel was already there, a mug of coffee in his hand, and the older police officer looked as if sleep mostly evaded him the night before.

"What happened to you?" Jared asked.

"My family happened to me," Mel said, glaring at Jared. "I was on the phone with various sisters until two in the morning because you arrested Harper. I have no idea how I got blamed for your actions ... but there it is."

"Your family seems awfully worried about what's going on with Harper Harlow," Jared pointed out. "Why is that? Is there some relationship I don't know about?"

"Harper is Zander's best friend," Mel replied.

"I know."

"They're thicker than thieves."

"I figured that out when I realized they were both in their late twenties and lived together," Jared said. "Don't you think they're a little old to be roommates?"

Mel sighed, exasperated. "You don't get it," he said. "They're not just friends ... they're *friends*."

"Did you just explain something to me?" Jared asked, confused.

"Those two have been joined at the hip since the moment they met," Mel said. "It was the first day of kindergarten. They took one look at each other and fell in love."

"This was obviously before Zander realized he was gay," Jared said, his tone dry.

"There are a lot of different kinds of love, son," Mel chided. "There are a lot of different kinds of soul mates. Zander and Harper are soul mates of a different kind. One day they'll find romantic soul mates, but they're always going to be soul mates of the friend variety."

"They're close," Jared said. "I get that. I don't understand why your family is up in arms about Harper. I can see them being upset because Zander is upset. This is something … different, though."

"Harper is a part of our family," Mel said. "Zander is a part of Harper's family. They're a unit. We all recognized that a long time ago. I can't explain why they're so close. Nothing in this world will ever tear them apart, though.

"Through the years it became expected to see them together," he continued. "Harper had presents under our family Christmas tree and Zander had presents under hers. When Gloria sent Harper to a girls-only summer camp the two of them went on a hunger strike until Phil picked her up and brought her home."

"That sounds a little co-dependent."

"It's more than a 'little co-dependent,'" Mel conceded. "They've shunned most other people who tried to be friends with them. Even when one of them is involved with someone else you can't separate them."

"That must be hard on the people they date," Jared mused.

"Harper doesn't really date," Mel said. "Not since … well … not in a few years."

Jared's interest was piqued. "Not since what?"

"She had a rough go of it a few years ago," Mel said, choosing his words carefully. "She was dating a guy named Quinn Jackson. They were pretty close. Zander even liked him. Then … well … his car was found down an embankment up on the bluff above the lake."

Jared's heart sank. "He died?"

"We think so," Mel said. "He's never been officially declared dead. The car was badly beaten up and the driver's side window was broken out like someone tried to climb out. There was blood all over the door and it was identified as Quinn's.

"Quinn's injuries would've been quite severe from the accident," he continued. "The working theory is he tried to climb out of the car and go for help, but that's pretty rough terrain out there. We think he died of internal injuries."

"You never found a body?" Jared was horrified.

"We looked for months," Mel said. "Harper kept going out there by herself. It wasn't that she didn't think Quinn was dead. She believed he was dead. She wanted a body to put him to rest, though. She wanted to make sure...."

"He wasn't wandering around as a ghost," Jared finished, his expression thoughtful. "How does your family feel about this whole ghost thing?"

"We love Harper," Mel replied. "We adore Zander. Zander adores Harper. My family believes."

"Do they really believe or do they just say they believe?" Jared couldn't let it go.

"Most of them really believe," Mel said. "You have to understand... Harper has proven herself so many times I've lost count. She's led us to bodies. She's saved lives. She's solved a lot of missing person cases."

"Why don't you believe?" Jared pressed.

"I don't know if I believe," Mel clarified. "I'm one of those people who has to see things for himself before it sinks in. I do believe Harper has special abilities. I'm not sure what they are, but she's not a normal girl."

Jared believed that. He barely knew her and couldn't help but see something "different" about her every time he was in close proximity. "When did she give up looking for Quinn?"

"Not for a long time," Mel said. "Finally ... one day she just let it go. She's never been the same since."

"I'm guessing Zander stood by her during all of this."

"Zander will stand by her until the day he dies," Mel said. "They're joined for life. Whoever finally manages to snag Harper – or Zander, for that matter – is going to have to realize that they're taking them both on."

"I didn't realize about the boyfriend," Jared said. "I feel kind of bad for hauling her in last night."

"She'll survive," Mel said. "She's strong."

"I guess."

"Can I ask you something?"

Jared arched an eyebrow and waited.

"How come you're so interested in Harper?" Mel asked. "Are you … attracted to her?"

"Of course not," Jared scoffed. "She keeps showing up at odd places and never has a good reason for being there. She showed up where a body was found, she went to the college to question people, she broke into a dead woman's house … all of those things make her suspicious."

"And yet I don't believe you're suspicious that she has anything to do with this," Mel said.

"I … she's a person of interest."

"Okay," Mel said, holding up his hands. "A courier is dropping off the autopsy. Let's focus on that and let Harper go back to … whatever it is she'll be doing today."

"That sounds like a great idea," Jared said, turning and heading toward the small kitchenette.

Mel watched him go, a small grin playing at the corners of his mouth. Harper Harlow may be a "person of interest" to Jared Monroe, but Mel had a feeling that *interest* was a lot more varied than even Jared understood.

"WELL, we can officially call it a homicide," Jared said, leafing through the medical examiner's findings. "Annie Dresden had sexual contact before her death and she was strangled."

"We can't be sure the sexual contact was involuntary," Mel warned.

Jared shot him a dubious look.

"She had sex with that nasty professor," Mel reminded him. "Just because they weren't seeing each other any longer that doesn't mean she wasn't seeing someone else."

"Don't you think the parents would've told us about that?" Jared pressed.

"The parents didn't know about the professor."

"You have a point," Jared said, rubbing the back of his neck to work out the kinks. While Mel was up late being lambasted by family members, Jared's lack of sleep came from his own fitfulness. He couldn't get the memory of Harper's red-rimmed eyes out of his mind the entire night. By the time his alarm dinged in the morning he'd only managed four total hours of sleep. He was exhausted. "The report says they're going to send the semen sample in for testing, but it could take some time to get the results back," Jared said. "They asked for a rush, but we both know how that goes."

"It's probably going to take at least a few days," Mel said. "We need to figure out where Annie disappeared from and work from there to find out where she was killed. I think it's fair to say she never made it back to her house."

"Those friends we interviewed yesterday said she was on her way to the library at six and the medical examiner puts her time of death around ten. That's only a four-hour window," Jared said.

"I'm going to assume she was in the library for at least an hour," Mel said. "I think we should head over there and see if we can find someone who remembers seeing her."

"That sounds like our best option for now," Jared agreed. "Let's get a move on."

"I KNOW ANNIE." One of the library workers, Lexie Marsden, fixed her wide eyes on Jared as she twirled a finger through her brown waves. She was attempting to flirt with the attractive police officer, but he was doing his level best to ignore her obvious "open for business" signals.

"Do you remember seeing her here three days ago?" Mel asked.

"She was here a lot, but I'm not sure I remember her … oh, wait, that's not true," Lexie said. "She was sitting at that table over in that corner." Lexie pointed. "I remember because she was one of the only ones here and I couldn't figure out why she wasn't out having a good time with everyone else."

"Her friends said she headed in this direction at around six," Jared said. "Does that sound right to you?"

Lexie racked her brain. "Yeah. I know she was still here around seven because that's when I take my break and I went out through the east door to smoke a cigarette. When I came back in I saw that she was packing up her stuff."

"That means she was getting ready to leave at seven-thirty. Is that right?" Jared pressed.

"I think it was closer to seven-forty-five," Lexie said, smiling sheepishly. "I took longer than I was supposed to on my break, but since the library was so empty I didn't think it would be a big deal."

"When Annie left, did she go out through the front door?"

"I have no idea," Lexie replied. "I wasn't paying attention."

"Did Annie talk to anyone while she was in here?" Mel asked.

"She was by herself and I didn't see anyone talking to her," Lexie said. "Was that helpful?"

"Very," Jared said, gracing her with a small smile.

"I … if you need anything else, you can call me whenever you want," Lexie said. "I mean … anything."

"Um, thank you," Jared said, shifting uncomfortably from one foot to the other.

Mel rolled his eyes. "Thank you so much for your time."

"Oh, one other thing," Jared said, turning back before he could move too far away from Lexie's eager countenance.

"Yeah?"

"Which way is the east door?" Jared asked.

"Right over there," Lexie said, working hard to hide her disappointment.

Instead of exiting the library through the door they entered Jared headed toward the side entrance Lexie indicated.

"What are you doing?" Mel asked, following close on his new partner's heels.

"I just ... I want to see something," Jared said, something Harper told him before leaving the station the previous evening echoing in his mind.

"What are we looking for?" Mel asked, pulling up short when he found Jared in the middle of the sidewalk outside of the library. "What are you looking at?"

"Doesn't Annie Dresden drive an older model Ford Explorer?" Jared asked.

Mel nodded.

Jared gestured toward one of only three vehicles in the well-hidden side lot.

"That looks like the vehicle we're looking for," Mel said, striding toward it. "How did you know to look over here?"

Jared didn't immediately answer. Instead, once he got to the driver's side of the vehicle, he played a hunch and hunkered down. There, just like Harper said he would, Jared found Annie's keys underneath the Explorer.

"We need a crime scene team out here," Jared said grimly.

"Tell me how you knew to look out here first," Mel prodded.

"Harper told me to before she left the station last night." It was hard to admit, but Jared wasn't big on lying.

"I told you she was special," Mel said, pulling his cell phone out of his pocket.

"I already knew that," Jared muttered. "Well ... crap."

FIFTEEN

"I heard you got arrested last night," Molly said, breezing into the GHI office a half hour late and fixing Harper with an excited look. "Did you get printed? Did they give you a chemical shower? Did you have to undergo a cavity search?"

Harper made a face from behind her desk. "You watch way too much television."

"Did any of that happen?" Molly asked, her enthusiasm shifting to disappointment.

"None of that happened."

"It's too bad, too," Zander said, winking at Molly. "There's nothing better than a good cavity search story."

"You're so funny," Harper deadpanned.

"How come you got arrested?" Eric asked, tapping his watch and giving Molly a pointed look.

"I'm not that late," Molly snapped.

"We don't have a job this morning so it doesn't matter," Harper said.

"It matters if I'm late," Eric said.

"We pay you," Zander replied.

"Barely," Eric muttered. He turned his attention back to Harper. "Why were you arrested?"

"I went to Annie Dresden's house hoping I could find her ghost," Harper explained. "I did and she asked me to look in the house to see if her bag was on the table. She couldn't remember if she made it home or not. She told me where to find the key and as I was letting myself into the house the cops showed up."

"That's rotten luck," Eric said. "Were you scared? I'll bet you were scared."

"It wasn't my finest moment," Harper conceded.

"Why didn't Annie just walk through the walls and look at the table herself?" Molly asked.

"Because I wasn't firing on all cylinders and didn't think that far ahead," Harper replied. "I was nervous ... and distracted ... and I was trying to keep Annie talking so I did as she asked."

"Was it the new cop?" Molly asked. "He's freaking hot, by the way."

"He is," Zander agreed.

"It was the new cop," Harper said, nodding. "He's not that hot."

"How come a Whisper Cove police officer arrested you at a St. Clair house?" Eric asked, his ever-pragmatic mind working overtime. "Is that even legal?"

"Technically she wasn't arrested," Zander said. "She was taken into custody for questioning and released without being arrested."

"He said he could arrest anyone if he caught them breaking the law and it didn't matter if he had proper jurisdiction or not," Harper said. "I'm looking that up, by the way. I'm not sure I trust him to tell the truth."

"I don't think he was lying," Zander said. "What does it matter now anyway? He let you go. No one is pressing charges. You didn't actually enter the house."

"He stopped you before you entered the house?" Eric asked, his eyes wide. "I wonder why. He would've had reason to hold you if you walked inside. By stopping you beforehand, he weakened his position."

Harper stilled, Eric's words washing over her. "I never really considered that."

"I told you he liked you," Zander teased. "He purposely stopped you from breaking the law because he didn't want to throw you in the big house. He was saving you."

"He does not like me."

"You think the new cop likes Harper?" Eric asked, his shoulders straightening.

"I hope he does," Molly said, shooting a small look in Eric's direction. His interest in Harper wasn't lost on her. "I think he and Harper would make a gorgeous couple."

"When did you see him?" Eric challenged.

"At the college the other day," Molly said. "He was talking to Harper and his body language said that he was hot for her."

"It did not," Harper scoffed.

Eric scorched Molly with a look. "When did you become an expert on body language?"

"I know when a guy is interested," Molly shot back. "This guy was interested in Harper. A girl can always tell these things."

"That's not true, is it?" Eric turned to Harper, a worried expression on his handsome face.

"A woman can always tell," Harper said, fighting the urge to roll her eyes at the triumphant look on Molly's face. "As a woman I can unequivocally tell you that Jared Monroe is not interested in me."

"You can't say that," Zander said. "You refuse to see what's right in front of you. He clearly finds you attractive … just like you find him attractive."

"You don't find him attractive, do you?" Eric was starting to get desperate.

"Not in the least," Harper said.

Eric looked relieved, if only marginally.

"That is such a load of crap," Zander said. "You might not be in love with him, but you're dying to see what he looks like without his shirt on."

"Lies!"

"I'm not the one lying," Zander said, his voice climbing to an almost shrill level. "You can't stop yourself from checking out his rear end every time you're around him. I know because I've been checking it out, too, and my eyes keep meeting your eyes there."

"That is ridiculous," Harper said.

Eric opened his mouth, and for a second Harper was worried he was going to blurt out a date invitation right then and there to head off another second of "hot cop" arguing. He never got the chance, though, and Harper would be forever thankful for the sound of someone clearing their throat at the front of the office.

Jared Monroe had his hands in his pockets as he shifted from one foot to the other by the front door. "I ... um ... your door was open."

Harper felt as if she'd been hit by a bus. All the air whooshed out of her lungs and her panicked eyes sought out Zander's for reassurance. He was too busy silently laughing to offer her any help, though.

Harper forced herself to her feet, her cheeks burning as she tried to decide how much of their childish argument Jared had overheard. "I ... can I help you?"

Jared licked his lips. He looked as nervous as Harper felt. "Can I talk to you in private for a few minutes?"

"Sure," Harper said, glancing around doubtfully. The office consisted of exactly one room and there was nowhere the two of them could go to avoid prying ears. "Maybe we should go outside?"

Jared looked relieved at the suggestion. "Sure."

Harper started to follow and then shot a quick look at Zander over her shoulder. "You can hold the fort down, right?"

Zander nodded, and when he was sure Jared's attention was focused elsewhere he mimed kissing an invisible person in front of him. Harper's cheeks grew even redder, but she refused to comment on what Zander was doing. Instead she followed Jared outside of the office – and toward what she was sure was certain doom.

JARED HAD no idea why he was so nervous but entering Harper's place of business put him on the defensive. It gave her a position of power. He believed that right up until the second he walked into the office and no one noticed him. Then he heard what they were arguing about and he couldn't stop himself from listening for a few minutes. He couldn't believe this group was considered professionals in any field.

He wordlessly led Harper to the small patio next to the office building and gestured toward the wrought iron table. Harper took one of the chairs and Jared settled in the other. He had no idea how he was going to start the conversation, but Harper didn't give him a chance to get his bearings.

"You found Annie's car, didn't you?"

Jared balked. "How did you know that?"

"I'm guessing," Harper said. "Did you think I was messing with you? Did you think a ghost told me? Did you think I was even crazier than you originally thought?"

Jared pinched the bridge of his nose to calm himself. He deserved that. He'd been condescending the night before. He'd treated her like a child. Now he was the one in the awkward position and she deserved her moment in the sun to gloat. "I ... I'm sorry," Jared said, the words sounding lame to his own ears.

"What are you sorry about?"

She wasn't going to make this easy on him. Jared didn't blame her. "I'm sorry you believe I think you're crazy."

"That's not an apology," Harper scoffed.

"I'm not sure what you want me to say."

"I'm not sure what I want you to say either," Harper said.

"Can we please start over?"

"I guess."

"We found Annie's car right where you said it would be," Jared said. "The keys were under the car."

"Did you find anything else?"

"Like?"

"Her bag," Harper said. "She was carrying a bag. Was it in the Explorer?"

"There was a bag in the backseat," Jared answered. "There was a textbook, a few notebooks, and gum inside."

Harper frowned. "What about an iPad?"

Jared shook his head. "Was there supposed to be an iPad inside?"

"Annie said there was," Harper said, racking her brain as she tried to remember the bulk of their conversation the previous evening. "I don't know what type it is or anything."

Jared glanced around the small patio. "Can't you just ask her?"

Harper made a face. "She's not here right now."

"Where is she?"

"She's not my shadow," Harper said. "She's not hanging around me twenty-four hours a day. I found her last night. She followed us to the police station. I haven't seen her since I left the station."

Jared considered the statement. "Do you think she'd be at the house if we went back?"

"We?" Harper's eyebrows nearly shot off her forehead. "Last night I was crazy and now we're working on this together? When did that happen?"

"I'm not saying we're working on this together," Jared cautioned. "I'm not even saying I believe all of ... this. I am saying I was wrong to dismiss you outright and I'm willing to listen to whatever you have to tell me. I ... that's the best I can do right now."

Harper tilted her head to the side, considering. "I guess that's fair," she said. "I can't ask you to believe me before I give you a reason to."

"Are you willing to go back to Annie's house with me and see if you can talk to her?" Jared couldn't believe he was asking the question.

"Are you going to arrest me if I do?"

Jared rolled his eyes. "Will you please let that go? I did not arrest you. I took you in for questioning."

"It cost me two hundred bucks to get my car back this morning," Harper said.

"If I write you a check will you come with me?" Jared's frustration was growing by leaps and bounds with each heated word. Unfortunately, his attraction to the annoying woman sitting next to him was growing at the same rate.

"I ... yes," Harper said, sighing as she gave in. As much as she wanted to give Jared a hard time, she wanted to help Annie more.

"Thank you," Jared said, surprised to find that he meant it.

"Do you want to go now?"

"Can we?"

"Sure. I need to tell Zander he's on his own for dinner and I'll pick up something on my way home," Harper said.

An idea occurred to Jared and before he had a chance to think better of it a suggestion was on the tip of his tongue. "We can eat dinner together."

SIXTEEN

Harper thought Jared was joking when he suggested they have a meal together, but after an hour of fruitless searching at Annie's house the duo gave up. Instead of driving Harper back to her office, though, Jared stopped at a local seafood restaurant on the lake.

Harper was floored. She didn't find her voice again until they were both seated with drinks in their hands.

"This is a nice place," she said, hoping her voice didn't give away her nervousness. "I … the food here is good."

"So I've heard," Jared said, his eyes scanning the menu. "I love seafood. I'm thinking I'm going to get this shrimp Pomodoro pasta dish."

"That's really good," Harper said, nodding. "I'll probably get that, too."

"You can get whatever you want," Jared said. "I'm buying."

"That's not necessary."

"Consider it a peace offering," Jared said.

After the waitress took their orders, Harper found herself searching for a conversation topic that wouldn't leave her feeling exposed. She decided that focusing on Jared was the way to go. "Why did you decide to take a job in Whisper Cove?"

Jared shrugged. "I grew up on the west side of the state, over by Kalamazoo," he said. "I like that area, don't get me wrong, but I always had the idea of working in a busier city going through my mind when I became a cop."

Harper snorted. "That doesn't explain how you ended up in Whisper Cove," she said. "Annie's murder notwithstanding, we're usually not a very happening place."

"It's not a great time to be a cop," Jared admitted. "Most of these local municipalities are cutting back. Whisper Cove had a job opening and it was close to the area I wanted to be in. The pay was good and the area was beautiful ... I decided to take it and see how things would work out."

"Did you buy a house?"

"I thought the Whisper Cove gossips would be all over that," Jared said, smirking. "I'm renting a house on the south side of town right now. It's a small ranch and I'm not in love with it or anything. Until I decide if this place is the right fit, I'm happy there, though. It's only a few blocks from the lake."

"Do you like the water?"

"I love the water," Jared said. "I like the sound of water as it's rushing into shore. I always thought it would be cool to live by an ocean, but I'm not sure if that will ever become a reality. What about you?"

"I love the lake, too. I go there every chance I get."

"Do you think you'll always stay in Whisper Cove?"

"I don't know," Harper said. "This is my home. I have a house here. I can't see myself leaving. Even though Whisper Cove is small it's only a half hour away from big box stores and malls. I'm pretty happy here."

"What about Zander?"

"Oh, Zander will never leave," Harper said, chuckling. "His mother would kill him."

"That's not what I mean," Jared said. "Do you think you'll always live with Zander?"

"Oh ... I don't know," Harper said. "He's my best friend."

"I know," Jared said. "I can tell how close you are. If he wasn't gay I would think you were a couple."

"If he wasn't gay we could never be friends," Harper corrected. "I would have to kill him for all the macho stuff he spouts."

"Why is it okay for him to spout it because he's gay?" Jared was genuinely curious.

"Because he's ... Zander," Harper said, her expression rueful. "I can't explain it. He's always been Zander and he's got a way about him that lets everyone in his life make excuses for the things he says and does. He's so charming people can't help but love him."

"That has to be hard on you, though," Jared said. "Eventually one of you is going to fall in love and want a permanent relationship. What happens then?"

Harper licked her lips, her mouth suddenly dry. "I don't know," she said after a moment of consideration. "Anyone in my life would have to understand that Zander is always going to be there. He's always going to be a huge part of my life."

"I don't doubt that," Jared said. "I would imagine your close bond with Zander is ... daunting ... for anyone interested in pursuing a relationship with you. Do you do that on purpose because of Quinn?"

Harper's heart rate increased and her face flushed with color. "What ... who ... why ... ?"

Her face was so red Jared was worried she was going to pass out. He fanned his hand in front of her. "Drink some water," he instructed. "I'm sorry I asked that. It's none of my business. I didn't realize you would react like this."

Harper took three huge gulps of water and then set the glass back down on the table, her hand shaking. Instinctively Jared reached across the table and placed his own hand on top of hers.

"I'm sorry," he said, his voice low. "I didn't mean to upset you."

"It's okay," Harper said, although she avoided meeting Jared's pointed gaze. "I didn't realize you knew about Quinn. It took me by surprise."

"I didn't until earlier today," Jared said. "I ... Mel told me. We were talking about me taking you into custody and he was explaining about your relationship with Zander and it kind of spilled out. Don't be angry with him."

"I'm not angry," Harper said. "I … it's public record."

"That doesn't mean you want people prying into your business," Jared said. "I can tell you're still messed up about it. You must have loved him very much."

Harper's eyes widened. "I cared about Quinn," she said. "I did. He was nice … and friendly … and he got along great with Zander."

"That's good."

"I wasn't in love with him, though," Harper said, her voice small.

Jared swallowed hard, confused how to proceed. "Mel made it sound like you fell apart when Quinn died," he said. "The way he talked … I thought … he said you spent months out there looking for Quinn's body so you could put him to rest."

"I would've done that for anyone," Harper said. "The idea of people wandering around aimlessly instead of moving on to their final resting place is troubling. I don't like it."

"Final resting place?"

"I guess it depends on what you believe," Harper said. "There's something else beyond the … wall … between here and forever."

"How do you know that?"

"I … it's just a feeling," Harper said, deciding now wasn't the time to admit she had a few another special ability besides talking to ghosts. "Unhappy spirits are the ones who stay behind. Murdered souls and tortured ghosts who were yanked out of their lives before they were ready to go often stay behind. Sometimes they need help to move on."

"And that's what you do?" Jared asked.

"That's what I try to do," Harper clarified. "It doesn't always work out how I would like, but most of the time we accomplish what we set out to do."

"You couldn't find Quinn when you went out there looking for him, could you?"

"How do you know I was looking for Quinn's spirit?" Harper asked.

"Because you strike me as someone who wants happy endings even if those endings lead to this ... other place," Jared said, internally marveling at how normal the conversation seemed despite the surreal nature of the words. "Why do you think you couldn't find him?"

"The truth?"

Jared nodded.

"In my head I picture Quinn's last hours being those of virtual torture," Harper explained. "Everyone agrees that any of the injuries he sustained in that accident would have left him in dire straits. He was strong enough to crawl out of the car window and then he died somewhere in the brush.

"He was alone and he was probably scared, but he was also in tremendous pain," she continued. "I'm guessing he knew he was dying and when it finally happened it was a relief because it meant he wasn't in pain any longer."

"If you believe that, why did you look for him for so long?" Jared asked.

"Because I had to be sure he wasn't wandering around lost somewhere," Harper said. "I didn't love Quinn when he died. We'd been dating about six months and I cared for him a great deal. I could've loved him eventually. I figured I owed him a few months of my life to make sure he wasn't holding on here when he could be in a happier place."

"That's a nice sentiment," Jared said. "I still believe part of you must have loved him to expend that much effort."

Harper shrugged noncommittally. "Maybe," she said. "I don't know. I know that losing him was hard. Zander never left my side, though. I believe Quinn is in a better place so I can live with his death."

"What about Annie?" Jared asked.

"Annie will move on soon," Harper replied. "She's ready, but she wants to help us find out who killed her. She doesn't want her murderer to kill someone else if she can stop him before it happens."

"Does she have any idea who hurt her?"

"No," Harper said. "She's worried she was raped, though. I'm worried, too. I think that might be the reason she's having so much trouble remembering."

"Why do you think that?" Jared asked, buying time so he could decide how much to tell her.

"She was found nude on the beach," Harper said. "Someone trying to hide semen and other fluids would dump a body in the lake as a forensic countermeasure. Annie doesn't have any ties to Whisper Cove."

"Maybe her killer does," Jared suggested.

"That's a possibility," Harper conceded, nodding. "Or maybe her killer has ties to Harsens Island, or New Baltimore, or Harrison Township. Just because Annie's body washed up on our beach doesn't mean she was killed in our waters."

"That's some pretty smart thinking there," Jared said, smiling.

"Zander and I watch a lot of television."

Jared snorted. "I'll bet," he said. "Can I ask you a few questions about seeing ghosts?"

"Yes."

"When you saw the first one, were you scared?"

"It was my grandfather and I was a child," Harper said. "I didn't know enough to be scared. He was in my bedroom and he was saying goodbye. I thought he was really there until my mother came in and told me what happened."

"What did you do?"

"I told them about our conversation, but they didn't believe me," Harper said. "It took a long time for them to realize I was telling the truth."

"Are you ever afraid?"

"Of ghosts?"

Jared nodded.

"I guess," Harper said, mulling the question over in her mind. "I'm more scared of not being able to help those who want it than I am of running into those who don't. Does that make sense?"

"I'm not sure any of this makes sense," Jared said. "I'm trying to feel the situation out as best I can."

"I guess I should consider that forward momentum," Harper teased, gracing him with the first real smile she'd been able to muster since he'd walked into her office. "It's hard for people who don't want to believe. Most of them can never cross the gap and become believers. I understand it. I do."

"What if I want to believe but still don't think I can?" Jared asked.

"Do you want to believe?"

Jared shrugged. He didn't have a simple answer. In truth, he found he was desperate to believe anything she told him. He was also struggling with the niggling worry in the back of his brain that she really was crazy. His heart, for whatever reason, refused to let him believe that, though. She was too earnest. She was too sweet. She was also too pretty and fiery. She was a compelling package. Unfortunately, it was one he didn't believe was meant for him. "I don't know what I want right now," he said finally.

"At least you're honest," Harper said, reaching for her water.

"I think that's my best virtue sometimes."

Harper couldn't help but agree even as she found hope coursing through her chest. Was there a chance he would ultimately give in and have faith in her? And, if he did, what would that mean in the grand scheme of things?

SEVENTEEN

"I can't believe I let you talk me into coming back here," Harper grumbled two hours later, her toe catching on the root of a tree and pitching her body forward.

Jared instinctively reached for her, catching her slight body in his arms before she could do any real damage. She flopped against him, her chest colliding with his, and Jared's arms were around her back before he realized what was happening.

"Oomph," Harper grunted, her eyes latching onto Jared's. "I... ."

Their mouths were only inches apart and Harper's heart was pounding so hard she was legitimately worried she was going to pass out. Her cheeks burned at Jared's proximity and yet she couldn't make herself pull away from him.

"Are you okay?" Jared asked, his voice low and husky as he rubbed his thumb against her back.

"I'm ... um ... I can't seem to remember what you just asked me," Harper murmured.

"Me either," Jared said. "I ... um ... what was I saying?"

Their gazes were fused together and Harper's hands, which were planted on Jared's firm chest, seemed to have a mind of their own as they wandered over the solid muscle under his shirt. "You work out."

"Five days a week."

If Harper didn't know better she would swear Jared's mouth was getting closer to hers. Her heartbeat sped up in anticipation. "I ... ." She was suddenly very aware of all the garlic in her pasta dish. *Oh, who cares?* He had garlic in his pasta dish, too, and she couldn't smell a thing.

Harper's world became myopically small and the only thing in it was Jared Monroe. The only thing she could feel were the hard muscles of his body. The only thing she could hear was blood rushing through her body. The only thing she could think about was his lips.

He was going to kiss her. This was the moment. It was going to happen. It ... .

"You're back," Annie said, popping into view and causing Harper to jerk in Jared's arms.

Even though the police detective couldn't see Annie he was sensitive enough to know something about Harper's demeanor had shifted. Jared took a quick step back, running his hand through his hair as he collected his wits. "I ... um ... are you okay?"

"I'm fine," Harper said, mimicking his movements with her own hair merely so she would have something to do with her hands. "I ... thank you for catching me."

"You could have hurt yourself," Jared said. "It was instinct."

"It also could have been really embarrassing," Harper said, shooting him a rueful smile. "Look at that. You saved me from possible broken limbs and your uncontrollable laughter when you saw me fall."

"I wouldn't have laughed."

Harper arched a confrontational eyebrow.

"Fine," Jared conceded. "I wouldn't have laughed until I was sure you weren't seriously hurt. Then I probably would've laughed until I cried."

"Well, at least your honest," Harper said, pressing her lips together.

"Oh, this is so ... hard to watch," Annie said, rolling her eyes.

"Do you have a problem?" Harper asked, shifting her attention to the irritated ghost.

"Who are you talking to?" Jared asked. "Is it Annie? Is she here?"

Harper nodded.

"What is she saying?" Jared pressed.

"So far she's making fun of us," Harper said. "The police found your car, Annie. The keys were right where you said they would be."

"So that wasn't a dream?" Annie asked, her eyes clouding.

"I'm afraid not," Harper said. "You left the library through the east door like you always do. What do you remember?"

"I don't have one clear memory," Annie replied. "It's more like I have ... several memory fragments."

"Tell me about them."

"I guess I should just stand here and let you handle this, right?" Jared asked, crossing his arms over his chest.

Harper ignored him and kept her focus on Annie. "Tell me," she prodded.

"I left the library and ... I remember looking up at the moon," Annie said. "It was a crescent moon and I remember thinking how big it looked."

"Okay," Harper said. "Then what?"

"I remember arriving at the Explorer and looking for my keys," Annie said, her eyes unfocused as she racked her tortured memory. "I think I put my bag in the back seat and then ... I'm not sure ... but I think I heard something behind me and that's it."

"The police found your bag where you left it," Harper said. "You told me your iPad was in it, though. Jared says it wasn't in the bag when they found it. That would mean someone took it. Are you sure it was in the bag?"

"I always carry it," Annie said. "It was in the bag. I'm positive."

"What did she say?" Jared asked, his patience wearing thin.

Instead of answering him Harper raised her index finger and continued talking to Annie. "Your autopsy results came back, too," Harper said, licking her lips. "Um ... do you want to know how you died?"

Annie's face was hard to read. She didn't particularly look

surprised by Harper's question, but she didn't exactly look thrilled with it either. "I was raped, wasn't I?"

Harper cleared her throat and shuffled from one foot to the other. "Yes."

"Don't look so sad," Annie said, her expression and tone flat. "I was found naked on a beach. I had a feeling that's what happened. I guess I didn't want to believe that's what happened ... but I knew."

"We don't know where your clothes are and your iPad being missing could be a clue," Harper said.

"Ask her where she bought the iPad," Jared suggested. "We might be able to find the serial numbers if we can track the purchase."

"She's not deaf," Harper said, shooting him a dark look. "She can hear you."

"I can't hear her, though, so it's weird holding one end of a conversation," Jared said. "Ask her."

"I heard him," Annie said before Harper could repeat the question. "It's a good thing he's so hot because otherwise ... ."

"Yeah, I have a feeling he's gotten through most of his life on his looks," Harper agreed.

"I heard that," Jared said. "I have no idea if I'm supposed to be angry or flattered, though, so I'm going to let it go."

"He's really adorable," Annie gushed, reaching over with her filmy hand and miming touching the side of his face.

Harper watched with unveiled interest as Jared swatted at his cheek. "Hurry up," he said. "The bugs are starting to come out. I thought it was a little early in the season for that but ... well ... I'm not a big fan of bugs."

Well, that was interesting. Harper tilted her head to the side as she considered the situation.

"He felt me," Annie said, her eyes widening in surprise. "He ... felt my hand."

"He did," Harper agreed. "Do it again. Pick a different spot."

"Pick a different spot for what?" Jared asked, confused.

Annie extended her index finger and poked it in the direction of Jared's lip. Jared's hand immediately came up and swatted the area.

LILY HARPER HART

"Isn't it too early for mosquitoes?" Jared complained. "I hate bug bites. Hurry up."

"It's not bugs," Harper said, reaching over and grabbing his hand so she could pull it away from his lip and get a better look. There was no mark there and yet he clearly felt Annie's touch.

"Did you know I could do that?" Annie asked.

"No," Harper said. "I know some spirits can affect physical things, but usually only clairvoyants and spiritualists can feel ghosts."

"What are you talking about?" Jared asked, frustration bubbling up.

"Can you feel ghosts?" Annie asked.

Harper nodded wordlessly.

As if to prove it to herself, Annie reached over and brushed her fingertips against Harper's forearm. Harper's arm broke out in goose pimples and she absent-mindedly let her fingers walk to the area in question.

"I guess it makes sense for you to feel it," Annie said. "You can see and hear me. How come he can feel it?"

That was a very good question. "I don't know," Harper said.

"Someone needs to tell me what's going on right now," Jared said, his voice taking on a hint of worry.

"You're not being bitten by bugs," Harper said. "Annie touched you … both times."

"She touched me?" Jared looked horrified. "Why?"

"The first time she touched you was because she thought you were hot."

"I am," Jared said, refusing to be charmed by the compliment. "Why did she do it the second time?"

"Because I asked her to," Harper replied, reaching over to grab his hand in an effort to offer comfort. "It's okay. She won't hurt you."

Instead of jerking his hand away, which was Harper's initial worry, Jared clasped her hand tightly. "This is freaking me out," he admitted. "I can't decide if this is really happening or if you're somehow hypnotizing me."

Harper barked out a hoarse laugh. "I can do a lot of things," she said. "Hypnotism isn't one of them."

Jared kept Harper's hand gripped tightly in his as he gathered himself. "Where did you get your iPad, Annie?"

Harper was bolstered by Jared's attempt to conform to the situation. He wasn't asking her to repeat things. He was taking it on faith that Annie could hear him, and for some reason that realization flooded Harper's body with warmth.

"I bought it at the Apple store at Partridge Creek," Annie said. "It's about six months old."

"Did you buy it in your name?" Harper asked.

Annie nodded. Harper could see she was only half-listening to the conversation. Her eyes had a far off quality that Harper recognized. Annie's mind was working hard and Harper couldn't help but wonder what she was thinking about.

"Was there anything on the iPad that someone would want?" Jared asked.

Annie snapped her attention back to the handsome police officer. "Like what?"

Jared didn't hear the question, but he must have anticipated it because he started talking before Harper could relay the message. "Was there a classroom assignment someone might have wanted? Was there financial information on it? How about any photographs that might worry people?"

"I did most of my assignments on my laptop," Annie said. "I don't have any financial information on it. The only thing with any monetary ties is the music and app store. As for photos ... ." Annie broke off.

"What is it?" Harper asked, sensing a change in the young woman's demeanor.

"There were some photos on it that one person would have a problem with," Annie said finally.

"What kind of photos?"

Jared watched what appeared to be a one-sided conversation with rapt interest and a closed mouth.

"I was dating a man for a few weeks," Annie started, choosing her words carefully. "He was a professor."

"Michael Dalton?"

"How did you know that?" Annie asked, stunned.

"We know about your relationship," Harper explained. "One of the other students saw you kissing him down by the pond. Dalton admitted the dalliance when Jared questioned him."

"Who told you that?" Jared asked. He was annoyed, but he didn't let go of Harper's hand. If she didn't know better, Harper would have thought he was using her presence to anchor him in a situation he never thought he'd find himself in.

"Mel told his sister."

"I'm going to have to kill Mel," Jared warned.

"You're going to have to get used to the fact that Whisper Cove is tiny and everyone gossips," Harper countered. She turned back to Annie. "Did you have photographs on your iPad of you and Professor Dalton ... doing stuff?"

"I had photographs of us doing a lot of stuff," Annie said. "I had photographs of us doing stuff that would be considered illegal in some countries."

"Oh, well, nice."

"What did she say?" Jared asked.

"I'll tell you later. Annie, did Professor Dalton know you had those photos?"

"Oh, he knew," Annie said. "When he dumped me in the dirt and treated me like a leper I threatened to show them to the dean. The dean looks the other way because most people don't complain about the stuff he does.

"I wasn't going to let him treat me like I was no better than some random slut he picked up on the street," she continued. "I told him I was going to show the dean the photos and get him fired."

"What did he say?"

"He said he was going to stop me," Annie said. "I thought he was being his usual obnoxious self ... but what if he wasn't?"

"I guess that officially gives him a motive," Harper mused. She quickly related Annie's information back to Jared. When she was done, she could practically see the gears in his mind working.

"Annie, did you have copies of those photos anywhere else?"

"They're on a flash drive in the shoebox on the top shelf of my closet," Annie said. "Everything you need is there."

"Annie, we don't know it's him," Harper cautioned. "He looks like a good suspect but ... ."

"It's him," Annie said. "He's the only piece of filth I know vile enough to do something like this. Go get the flash drive. Nail his ass to the wall."

"Where are you going?" Harper asked, worried.

"I'm going to see if I can touch Professor Dalton," Annie replied, her tone grim. "I think we have a few things to work out."

Before Harper could caution her about her plan of action Annie blinked out of sight. "Uh-oh."

EIGHTEEN

By the time Jared and Mel hit the St. Clair Community College campus the next morning the whole case had been turned on its head.

"I don't understand how you got this lead," Mel pressed, struggling to keep up as Jared strode toward the building where Professor Michael Dalton's office was housed.

"I ... it's complicated," Jared said, refusing to meet his partner's studied gaze.

"Does this have something to do with Harper Harlow?"

Jared slowed his pace. "Why would you ask that?"

"Because I happen to know you showed up at GHI yesterday and asked her out on a date," Mel said.

"I did not ask her out on a date," Jared said. "I asked her to help me with something and it just so happened to overlap with my dinner hour so we had something to eat. What is GHI?"

"Ghost Hunters, Inc. is the name of Zander and Harper's business," Mel said. "Where did you go for dinner? Was it some place romantic?"

"It was some seafood place on the lake," Jared said. "Ghost Hunters, Inc.? Really? That's a pretty lame name."

"I think Ghostbusters was already taken," Mel said, his tone dry. "Are you and Harper a thing now?"

"We had dinner and we talked," Jared said firmly. "We got off on the wrong foot and I felt bad about that whole taking-her-into-custody thing after finding out about the boyfriend."

"Did you talk about Quinn?" Mel asked, his eyebrows lifting.

"A little."

"I'm impressed," Mel said. "Harper doesn't usually talk about Quinn with anyone except Zander. She must trust you."

The words took Jared by surprise. "She was ... unhappy ... when I mentioned him. She talked about him a little after that, though."

"You like her," Mel said, grinning. "You've gone from a non-believer to a believer and you like her."

"I do not like her. She's a nice woman who has the potential for helping with a murder investigation. That's all."

"Zander said you liked her and I thought he was making it up," Mel said, rubbing his chin. "The boy is prone to dramatic fits sometimes so I thought he was exaggerating. He wasn't, though. You like her."

"I don't even know her," Jared argued.

"I didn't say you were in love with her," Mel said. "It's perfectly okay to like a woman. Harper is ... beautiful. She's a good kid. She's got a great heart. You know she's fragile, though, right? She's still getting over Quinn."

Jared had no idea why but Mel's words irked him. "She says she was never in love with Quinn."

Mel was taken aback. "She told you that?"

"She said they were happily dating and relatively close, but she wasn't in love with him," Jared said, flustered that he was even arguing the point. "She said it could've grown into a case of love, but they never got the chance."

"It sounds like the two of you had quite the conversation," Mel said. "When are you going out again?"

"We're not dating!"

Mel smirked. "Not yet. Oh, this is priceless. I can't wait until this news hits town. Harper Harlow has been the most sought after woman in her age bracket for … I don't know how long. Now here you come swooping into town and the first thing you do is start dating everyone's resident crush. That's hilarious."

"I'm not telling you this again," Jared said, extending his finger in Mel's direction. "We're not dating."

"You went with her to talk to a ghost last night," Mel argued. "Yesterday morning you didn't believe in ghosts. In less than twenty-four hours you've done a complete turnabout and now we're going to question a murder suspect on the word of a ghost."

"I … it can't hurt to question him," Jared said. "I don't know what I believe."

"Harper is magic, son," Mel said. "I don't know if I believe in ghosts either, but I do believe in her. There's no shame in it. People in town have faith in her for a reason. No one is going to fault you for believing in her."

"What if I fault myself?"

"That's something you're going to have to tackle on your own," Mel said. "Now, come on. Let's go talk to the resident dirtbag and see what he has to say for himself. Something tells me it's not going to be anything good."

Jared followed Mel wordlessly. Something told him that his new partner was right about more than just Michael Dalton. He couldn't get Harper out of his mind and it was starting to drive him crazy.

MOLLY WAS in the middle of a righteous meltdown as she paced in front of Harper's desk.

"The whole night all he did was talk about you. The whole night!"

Harper knew she was talking about Eric without having to ask the obvious question. "Molly, I don't know what you want me to say," she said. "Eric has a crush on me. It won't last."

"That's what you said six months ago."

"It's still true."

"Are you sure you're not interested in him?" Molly asked,

narrowing her eyes suspiciously as she planted her hands on her hips. "You can tell me. I won't get angry."

Harper didn't believe that for a second. Since she wasn't interested in Eric, though, she saw no sense in lying. "I'm sure."

Molly visibly relaxed. "Are you interested in Jared?"

Harper's shoulders involuntarily stiffened. "Of course not."

"I think you are," Molly said. "You should've seen your face when he walked into this office yesterday. It was like your pants were on fire – and not because you were going to lie to him, if you know what I mean?" Molly waggled her eyebrows suggestively.

"I know what you mean," Harper said, making a face. "I also know that I'm not even remotely interested in Jared."

"Zander says you are."

"Zander also maintains that Betty White isn't the only surviving member of *The Golden Girls* and that a reunion is still possible if someone could just uncover the conspiracy," Harper pointed out.

"That's Zander being funny," Molly said, her face serious. "Zander knows you better than anyone else in this world and he says you're hot for the new cop."

"Zander is going to be hot when I'm done beating him with a belt," Harper grumbled.

"It's okay to like Jared," Molly said. "I know you don't really date and you've been pretty obvious about putting Eric off but … it's okay. You're allowed to like Jared."

"I'll take that under advisement," Harper said. She lifted her eyes to Molly's and internally debated about continuing the dating discussion. She knew it was a bad idea, but she plowed ahead anyway. "If we're going to talk about relationships and crushes I think it's only fair that we talk about your situation."

"I don't have a situation," Molly said, feigning a look of contrition on her face. "I'm an open book and I don't mind talking about your dating life, but I don't have one."

"That's because you've set your sights on Eric," Harper replied, refusing to let the fast-talking Molly derail the conversation. "You know he's not into you, right?"

"I don't have a crush on Eric," Molly sniffed, crossing her arms over her chest. "I don't care about him at all. He's merely a co-worker – and an obnoxious one at that."

Harper licked her lips as she decided how to proceed. "Everyone knows you have a crush on Eric. Eric knows you have a crush on him. He's not open to a relationship, though. I think you would do better to turn your attention to someone your own age."

"I don't have a crush on Eric!"

"Don't get all … petulant," Harper chided. "You have a crush on Eric. It's not a crime. I think you would have a better chance with him if you dated someone else and weren't always so … available … to help him."

"I'm not available," Molly countered. "I like the technical aspects of what we do. He's the one most knowledgeable when it comes to the computer stuff. That's the only reason I hang around him."

"Fine," Harper said, holding up her hand in a placating manner. "You don't have a crush on Eric."

"Thank you."

"Just like he doesn't have a crush on me," Harper added.

Molly scowled.

"Honey, you're very pretty and you could have almost any guy you want," Harper said, taking a sisterly approach with her young protégé. "If you date someone else you might give Eric the chance to realize that you're a catch and he might actually be interested in catching you."

Molly looked intrigued at the suggestion. "Go on."

"Eric thinks he doesn't want you because you want him," Harper elaborated. "Men like the chase. Date someone else and make Eric realize you're not going to sit around waiting for him. Make him realize he should want to chase you."

"Do you have anyone in mind?"

"What about Collin? He seems like a nice guy."

"He does seem like a nice guy," Molly mused. "He's cute, too."

"He's definitely cute," Harper agreed. "I'm not saying you have to throw yourself into a relationship with Collin, but if you made a date with him and he happened to pick you up when Eric was here that might work in your favor."

"That's a really good idea," Molly said, jumping to her feet. She was obviously over denying she had a crush on Eric. "That's what I'm going to do."

"Good for you. Just make sure you stay away from his brother. That kid is a dirtbag."

Molly shuffled toward the door, turning back swiftly when a thought occurred to her. "Is that how you're going to snare Jared? Are you going to make sure he sees you out on a date with another man?"

"For the last time, I am not interested in Jared!"

"How come you can see when everyone else has a crush and yet you can't recognize it in yourself?"

PROFESSOR DALTON was haughty when Jared and Mel walked into his office. "I told you to call my attorney if you had more questions," he said.

"We can do that," Jared said. "I thought you would want us to talk this over with you before going to the press, though."

"Press? What are you talking about?"

Jared held up the flash drive he'd found inside Annie's closet the night before. "Annie Dresden had photographs of the two of you in bed ... and on the kitchen table ... and on the lawn of the library," he said. "We know she was threatening you with going to the dean."

"I ... so what?"

"That gives you motive to kill her," Mel said. "We've taken DNA samples from Annie's body. They're at the lab now. The photographs are enough to formally haul you into the station for questioning, though."

"I didn't kill her," Dalton said, his lower lip quivering. "I don't care what you think. I'm a sex fiend. I admit it. I'm not a nice guy. I'm also not a murderer."

"Sir, you had a sexual relationship with a student who was threatening to go public," Mel said. "That student showed up raped and murdered on a local beach. We've done some research and found that you keep a boat out at the St. Clair Marina. That gives you motive and means."

"You also don't have an alibi," Jared pointed out.

"I'm not a murderer," Dalton said, all signs of bravado missing. "I swear. I never hurt Annie. I wouldn't do that."

Jared sighed and ran a hand through his hair. "Professor Dalton, we're going to have to ask you to accompany us to the Whisper Cove Police Department for formal questioning."

"I want a lawyer!"

"That's your prerogative," Mel said. "You're not under arrest right now. If you refuse to cooperate, though, we will have to put you in custody."

"I'm going to sue your whole department!"

Jared was done messing around. "Sir, please get to your feet and place your hands behind your back. Don't make this any more difficult than it has to be."

NINETEEN

"Don't burn those steaks," Harper ordered later that evening, glancing over Zander's shoulder as he manned the grill on their side patio.

"When do I ever burn the steaks?"

"At least three out of every five times you cook them."

"I'm offended," Zander said, waving the tongs he was holding in Harper's face. "I am the best cook in this house."

"You wish," Harper scoffed.

"Honey, you burnt cereal the other morning."

"You don't cook cereal."

"And yet you still burned it," Zander said. "It was disgraceful."

The look Harper sent Zander was almost comical and Jared couldn't hide his laugh as he watched them cavort. They both jerked at the noise, swiveling quickly to find him standing at the edge of the patio watching them. "Hi," he said.

"Hi," Harper said, exhaling heavily. "I … um … we're usually not this immature."

"She's lying," Zander said. "We're always this immature. Do you want to stay for dinner? I have another steak in the refrigerator."

Jared was surprised by the offer. "I ... um ... sure," he said, squaring his shoulders. "That sounds nice. Are you sure I'm not intruding?"

"I'm sure," Zander said, not bothering to fight the grin spreading across his face when he got a gander at Harper's flustered countenance. He handed the tongs to her. "Watch the steaks while I go get one for Officer Monroe."

"You can call me Jared."

"Welcome to our home, Jared."

Once Zander made himself scarce, Jared and Harper were alone – and wildly uncomfortable with the situation.

"I shouldn't have just shown up like this," Jared offered by way of apology. "It was rude, but I had something I wanted to tell you and I realized I didn't have your phone number."

Harper narrowed her eyes. "You have Mel's phone number."

"So?"

"Everyone in Zander's family has my phone number," Harper said. "I think you came by because you wanted to see me." The words were out of her mouth before she could give reasonable thought to the intelligence behind them.

Jared was surprised by her words, but he couldn't deny their truth. "Maybe I did want to see you," he conceded. "I ... can't explain it. I haven't been able to think about anything but you all day."

Harper's cheeks warmed at his admission. "I ... um ... hmm."

"I'm going to bet you're rarely speechless so I'm going to guess that you weren't expecting me to say that," Jared said. He rolled up his sleeves and took the tongs from her, edging her over with his hip so he could have room to maneuver in front of the grill. "You're going to burn those steaks."

Harper had no idea what to say so she let her mouth hang open in the hope that a smart comeback would magically form on her lips.

"The trick is to make sure the meat isn't bloody without burning the exterior," Jared said, focusing on the steaks. "You have the heat up too high."

"That's what you have to say?" Harper asked, finally finding her voice. "That's what you have to say after you tell me you've been thinking about me all day?"

"What do you want me to say?" Jared asked, his blue eyes thoughtful as they landed on her matching set. "You told me last night you liked me because I told the truth. The truth is my mind has wandered to you and what you were doing about eight hundred times today."

"I don't know what to say to that," Harper said, her voice shaking. "I ... ."

"Mel gave me an earful about you this morning," Jared said, not letting Harper get ahead of him in the conversation. "He said he heard we went on a date and he wanted to know how it went. I said we weren't on a date and he claims we were.

"Then I started thinking about it and realized it kind of felt like a date," he continued, using the tongs to prod the meat on the grill. "After I realized it was kind of a date I tried to decide how I felt about it. When I couldn't come up with an answer, I asked myself how I would feel if I saw you on a date with another man.

"I didn't like that idea at all," Jared said. "The thing is, I've been in this town for exactly seven days. I don't know anything about you other than you're beautiful and you talk to ghosts. I'm not sure I'm ready to date you."

"Who says I want to date you?" Harper challenged.

"Your face," Jared replied, unruffled. "We were both in Annie Dresden's yard last night and we both know what was about to happen if she hadn't shown up. Are you going to deny it?"

"I ... ."

"Holy crap! What almost happened in Annie Dresden's yard last night?" Zander barreled back out onto the patio, a cellophane-wrapped steak clutched in his hand. "You've been holding out on me, missy. You said nothing happened. Now I'm eavesdropping and hear something almost happened. Spill!"

Jared wanted to be annoyed with Zander's appearance – and he partially was – but he was also relieved because the look on Harper's face a few moments before told him she was about to dig her heels in and deny the combustible chemistry that sparked whenever they were in close proximity to one another. Jared wasn't sure if he could take that. Zander's appearance gave him time to think.

"Nothing happened," Harper sputtered. "You're overreacting."

Zander turned to Jared for confirmation. "You tell me what almost happened."

Jared was unsure how to proceed. "Um ... ."

"If you want to date her you're going to need me on your side," Zander said. "I'm going to be the best ally you've ever had. I need to know I can trust you, though."

That was an interesting proposition. "She tripped over a root and almost fell," Jared said. "I caught her and there was a moment when we were pressed up against each other where I gave serious thought to kissing her."

"How did she respond?" Zander asked.

"She almost kissed me back," Jared said. "Then Annie Dresden showed up and the moment was ruined. We both pretended it didn't happen. The problem is: I haven't been able to think about anything but her since then."

"I like your honestly," Zander said. He unwrapped the steak and handed it to Jared. "Do you want to kiss her?"

"I definitely want to kiss her," Jared said. "I'm not sure about after that, though."

Zander narrowed his eyes. "We don't take kindly to the 'wham, bam, thank you, ma'am' sorts in this house," he warned. "Is that the type of guy you are?"

Jared snickered. "Not last time I checked."

"When was your last serious relationship?" Zander asked.

"I ... ." Jared broke off, not sure how to respond.

"It's not a trick question."

"I know," Jared said. "It's just ... I'm not sure I've ever dated anyone seriously. I've had girlfriends, but none of them have stuck around for all that long."

"Why? Are you bad in bed?"

Jared's cheeks burned as Harper covered her eyes in mortification. "I hope not," he said. "None of the feedback I've received in that department has been of a negative variety. Well, I'm sure my high school game wasn't great, but I've learned a few things since then."

"Do you sleep with women and never call them?" Zander asked.

"No. In fact, I usually like to get to know a woman before I sleep with her."

"That's a good answer," Zander said. "How well endowed are you?"

"Zander!" Harper scorched her best friend with a harsh look.

"I'm asking for me just as much as her," Zander explained. "I like to get the full picture when I imagine someone naked."

"I'm not answering that," Jared said.

"What are your intentions with Harper?"

"I honestly have no idea," Jared replied. "I'm not sure I can wrap my head around this whole ghost thing and yet I can't stop thinking about her. That's as much thought as I've given this."

"Why did you come over here?" Zander pressed. "Were you hoping she would be alone so you could kiss her?"

"I wouldn't have minded that, but in reality I had news about Professor Dalton and instead of tracking down her phone number – which was in the computer system on my desk – I decided I wanted to use the information about the professor as an excuse to see her."

"That's another good answer," Zander said. "I like you."

"I'm glad," Jared said. "My understanding is if I am going to want to date Harper I'm going to need your seal of approval beforehand."

"You didn't ask for it last night," Zander reminded him.

"That's because I didn't realize last night was a date."

"It wasn't a date," Harper hissed.

"Shut up and let us talk," Zander chided her. "You know Harper is my best friend in the world, right?"

Jared nodded.

"I'll have to kill you if you hurt her," Zander warned.

"I don't want to hurt her," Jared said. "I know that. I'm not even sure if I want to date her. Well, that's not true. I definitely want to date her. I guess it's more that I'm not sure if it's smart to date her."

"Because of your job? Are you worried people will laugh at you for dating a ghost hunter?"

"I don't really care what people think about me," Jared countered. "I ... I'm not sure if Whisper Cove is going to be my forever home and I think she's definitely sure it is going to be her forever home. That might throw a kink into things."

"Oh," Zander said, making a face. "That's very pragmatic of you."

"I can't help it. That's the way I was born."

"Well, I know a little something about that," Zander said, rubbing the back of his neck as he turned to Harper. "I think you should give him a shot. You're obviously into him and he's really into you. I don't want to see you get hurt, but I have a feeling you can make him fall in love with you and he'll never want to leave Whisper Cove."

"Zander!" Harper was beside herself.

"You have my approval to date her," Zander said, ignoring Harper. "You need to try to wrap your head around the ghost stuff, though. It's never going to change and she's the real deal."

"I think I've already come to that conclusion myself," Jared said, smiling at Harper ruefully.

"Let's eat," Zander said. "You can tell us all about your afternoon with that smarmy professor."

"I can't wait," Jared said, his eyes soft as they searched Harper's face.

"Me either," Harper muttered.

TWENTY

"Have you arrested Dalton?" Harper asked, handing the steak sauce to Jared. The police officer was sandwiched between Harper and Zander and yet he didn't appear to be bothered by the intense interest of either one of them.

"Not technically," Jared said. "We brought him down for formal questioning and he pitched an absolute fit about being railroaded."

"Do you believe him?"

"I don't know," Jared said truthfully. "The guy is a world-class worm of the nastiest order, but guys like him usually don't kill women."

"What about the photos? Did you look at the flash drive?"

"I looked at the photos," Jared said. "The guy is into some ... freaky ... stuff."

"Whips and chains?" Zander asked sagely.

"More like weird places and public settings," Jared replied, sawing into his steak. "This looks good."

"You're the one who ended up cooking it," Zander said. "If you're going to be hanging around here with us you should probably know now that Harper can't cook. If you want breakfast in the morning you're going to have to wait for me to cook it."

Jared was tickled by Zander's forthright nature. "Thanks for the heads up. I'll keep that in mind when I start spending the night here."

"I love your attitude, man," Zander said.

"Doesn't anyone want to hear what I have to say about the possibility of Jared spending the night here?" Harper asked.

"No," Zander said. "Eat your corn and steak. If you can't say anything nice then you should keep your mouth shut. This is the best nibble you've had in ... well ... a long time."

"Since Quinn," Harper said. "Go ahead and say it. It's not a dirty word."

"Harper ... ." Zander's face twisted.

"He already knows about Quinn," Harper said, her voice low. "Mel told him."

"Oh," Zander said, shifting his attention to Jared. "My family is full of people with big mouths. You should know that, too."

"I figured that out my first day on the job," Jared said. He wasn't looking at Zander while he was talking to him, though. Instead he was fixated on Harper. He reached over and rubbed her shoulder, the gesture instinctive. "I'm not sure how much you want me to talk about Quinn. It seems like a sore subject."

"It's not a sore subject," Harper said. "In fact, I wish people would bring him up more often. People are terrified to talk about him with me."

"You can talk about him with me," Jared said. "Did I put up a fight last night when you opened up?"

"You opened up?" Zander was flabbergasted. "Who are you and what have you done with my Harper?"

"You don't have to be so dramatic," Harper said. "I just told him that I wasn't in love with Quinn and I was hopeful he was in a better place."

"That's a big deal for you," Zander said. "I'm proud."

"Ugh, I can't even look at you right now."

Jared smirked. "If you start dating me you might be able to convince me to beat him up for you from time to time," he offered.

Harper couldn't help herself and she burst out laughing. "You're playing both of us. Nice."

"You could never take me," Zander scoffed. "I work out five days a week."

"I'll go to the gym with you and we can box," Jared offered.

"Zander doesn't go to a gym like that," Harper said, giggling. "He goes to a gym where everyone manscapes and they're only half there to work out."

"Ah," Jared said. "Well, we can still go to the gym together. We'll have a competition to see who can bench press more."

"I seriously love this guy," Zander enthused. "If you don't date him I'm going to."

"I'm pretty sure you're not my type," Jared deadpanned. "I don't care how much you manscape. I'm not interested in the parts you're offering."

"You're cute," Zander said. "I ... ."

"Can we please turn the conversation back to something important?" Harper asked, her irritation bubbling up.

"Yes, my queen," Zander said. "She has PMS. Just FYI."

"Thanks for the 4-1-1," Jared said.

Zander snorted as Harper rolled her eyes.

"Can't you please finish your story about Professor Dalton before you two start flexing your muscles?" Harper asked.

"Sure," Jared replied. "There's honestly not much to tell. We showed him the photos. He didn't deny them. He did deny going after Annie. He said he would never do that. Then he lawyered up and we had to let him go."

"Why didn't you arrest him?" Harper asked.

"We don't have any evidence," Jared said. "We have suspicious behavior on his part, but we don't have the DNA results on the semen sample found inside of Annie yet and we don't have any other forensic evidence because the water washed it all away. We need a break – and I'm not sure where we're going to get it from."

"Do you think it's him?" Harper asked, her face serious.

"I want to think it's him," Jared said. "The guy is a user and manipulator. I can't say I really and truly believe it's him, though."

"What do you do next?"

"Finish my dinner," Jared said. "Then I thought I would enjoy some more of Zander's delightful company. You can hang around, too, if you want."

"Oh, he's a keeper," Zander said.

"I was talking about with the case," Harper snapped.

"I know," Jared said. "I don't know where to go with the case. I'm hoping Annie remembers what happened to her. We can't use her as a witness in court, but at least it would give us a solid place to focus."

"What happens if she never remembers?" Zander pressed.

"Does that happen?" Jared asked.

Harper shrugged. "Sometimes. She's remembering bits and pieces, though. I think she's eventually going to remember."

"I hope it's sooner rather than later," Jared said. "I don't like the idea of a predator walking free and knowing he could do something to another innocent girl."

"I don't like it either," Harper said.

"I know," Jared said. "I want to solve this case. Until we do, I'm afraid I can't plan our first date. You're going to have to pine for me for a few more days it seems."

"You're pretty full of yourself," Harper said, arching an eyebrow.

"Don't worry. I promise I can back it up." Jared winked at her playfully.

"I'm officially in love with him," Zander said.

"**THIS** IS A NICE HOUSE," Jared said, looking around the kitchen with obvious interest. "Did it come like this or did you two do a lot of work on it?" He was leaning against the counter with a beer in his hand as he watched Zander and Harper load the last of the dinner dishes into the dishwasher.

Zander snorted. "Harper does not do home improvement projects."

"I can do ... crafty things," Harper argued.

"Honey, you failed home economics because you couldn't thread the sewing machine," Zander reminded her.

"That's because those machines were ancient," Harper said. "Besides, I'm sorry, there should be an easier way to thread a machine. We have all the technology in the world and yet that is still like medieval torture."

Jared smiled. "You don't strike me as the crafty sort."

"I can craft with the best of them," Harper said, grabbing Jared's beer from his hand and taking a proprietary swig from it.

"That's cute," Zander said. "You're already sharing beverages."

"Shut up," Harper said. "I ... ." She broke off when she heard the back door open. Everyone shifted their attention in the direction of the door and when Phil stomped into the room only Jared appeared surprised.

"Women are evil devils!" Phil opened the refrigerator door and rummaged around, not returning until he had his own beer. "I'm not talking about you, honey. You're the only woman in this world who shouldn't be stabbed and buried alive."

"You say the sweetest things, Dad."

"I'm not joking, though," Phil said. "I'm done with women. I never want to see another one again." He twisted the top off the beer and took a long swig.

"I know some nice men you might like," Zander offered.

"Don't be cute," Phil said. "I said I was off women. I didn't say I was on men."

"You don't know what you're missing," Zander said.

Phil made a face. "We've talked about this," he said. "I'm perfectly fine with your lifestyle and whatever it is that you want to do. You promised to never talk to me about it, though."

"Dad ... ."

Phil ignored his daughter. "Don't you want to know why I'm off women?"

"No," Harper answered.

"Yes," Zander said, nodding vigorously as he ignored the death glare Harper lobbed in his direction. "I always love your dating stories."

"I thought you said that people shouldn't date until their divorces were finalized," Harper reminded him.

"I say a lot of things, Harper," Phil shot back. "Most of them don't stick because I'm fickle and I lie to get my own way sometimes."

Jared pursed his lips to keep from laughing out loud. Despite not being formally introduced he'd managed to ascertain that Phil was not only Harper's father, but also a hilarious source of entertainment.

"What was wrong with your date tonight?" Zander asked, feigning sympathy.

"I went out with Margo Fields," Phil said.

Zander guffawed. "Doesn't she have a yard full of ceramic geese?"

"And a house full of cat needlepoint," Phil said. "It was frightening. I thought I was walking into a pet store except everything was pastel and covered in plastic."

Harper wrinkled her nose. "Plastic?"

"Yeah, she had one of those plastic covers over her couch," Phil said. "I knew there was something wrong with that woman when she asked me out."

"I think that was the first clue for all of us," Harper deadpanned.

"I spent five minutes with her tonight and I wanted to deafen myself with Q-tips," Phil said. "She cooked something that looked as if it might have been cat at one point."

"How did you leave things?" Zander asked. "You didn't tell her you would call her again, did you?"

"Oh, she doesn't think I'm going to call her," Phil said. "I excused myself to go to the bathroom and crawled out the window. I'm pretty sure she realizes that means I won't be calling for another date."

Harper's mouth dropped open as Zander slapped the counter because he was laughing so hard. Harper risked a glance at Jared and found his shoulders shaking with silent laughter. "That is horrible, Dad," Harper chided. "That poor woman … what is she going to tell people?"

"That her cats scared me away," Phil said. "She can't honestly think any man is ever going to think that's okay."

"You're a terrible person," Harper said, reaching for Jared's beer again. He handed it to her wordlessly.

"Who are you?" Phil asked, finally focusing on Jared.

"I'm Jared Monroe."

Phil shook Jared's proffered hand and looked him up and down. "I apologize for not introducing myself sooner," he said. "I assumed you were one of Zander's friends and that I would never see you again once he decided you had too much ear hair or whatever his new dating issue is this week."

"His date this week talked with his mouth full of food," Harper offered.

"You're not here because of Zander, though," Phil said. "You're here for my daughter."

Jared stilled, surprised by the statement. "I . . . ."

"Who told you that?" Harper asked.

"Everyone in town is talking about how you went on a date with this guy last night."

"It was not a date," Harper growled.

"How did they even know?" Zander asked.

"Haddie Lewis was at the same restaurant," Phil said. "She told everyone at the senior center this afternoon that Jared and Harper looked very cozy."

"That's a lie," Harper protested.

Phil studied Jared for several moments and then shrugged. "You'll do. If you've managed to gain my daughter's interest you have to be doing something right and I won't have ugly grandchildren if you two are responsible for them.

"I officially welcome you to my family," Phil said, extending his hand.

Harper arched an eyebrow as Jared risked a quick glance in her direction. "Oh, yeah, I'm not looking like much of a prime dating option now, am I?"

Jared tilted his head to the side, considering. "If anything I'm finding you more and more attractive."

"I seriously love you," Zander gushed.

Harper was worried her best friend was going to have to get in line where that sentiment was concerned because the more time she spent with Jared Monroe the more she realized she couldn't stop thinking about him either.

Her whole life was spinning out of control.

TWENTY-ONE

"I think we should go back to the college," Harper announced the next morning.

Zander looked up from his coffee, a blank look on his face, and immediately started shaking his head. "Why?"

"Because Annie Dresden is still wandering around as a ghost," Harper explained. "She can't be put to rest until her murder is solved."

"And Jared told you last night he's not going to ask you out until the murder is solved, too," Zander said.

"That has nothing to do with anything."

"Don't you even bother lying to me," Zander scolded her. "You didn't tell me about the almost-kiss or the fact that you talked to him about Quinn. I feel so ... betrayed ... as it is. If you lie to me about this I'm going to have to end our friendship."

They both knew it was an empty threat.

"Zander ... ."

Harper's face was so earnest Zander couldn't take it. "It's okay, Harp," he said. "You can like him. You're allowed. He's a nice guy. He's handsome. He's funny. He obviously has great taste in women. Please don't ruin this chance before you even see if you can like him."

"I don't want to ruin this chance," Harper admitted. "I ... I've been thinking about him, too. Ever since I met him. There's something about him ... I can't put my finger on it ... but it's as if I'm drawn to him."

"Good," Zander said. "You deserve a little happiness."

"What if he breaks my heart?"

"You can't go through life scared to try the things that might make you happy because they also might make you sad," Zander said. "That's not how this world works, love of my life. The best things in life come with risks."

"What if he never accepts that I can see ghosts?"

"He already does," Zander said. "He wouldn't have come to the house if he thought you were a loon."

"He doesn't know about the other part, though," Harper pointed out. "He doesn't know I can ... see the other side."

"Give it time before you tell him that," Zander said. "I've loved you my whole life and I still have trouble with that. It's going to be okay. I feel it here." He tapped the spot on his chest above his heart. "You need to open yourself up and let him get to know you. I'm not saying he's going to be your forever, but I do think he's got a shot of making you really happy."

"He said himself he doesn't think he wants to stay in Whisper Cove."

"That's what you heard because you were looking for a reason to let him go," Zander countered. "Even if he gets a job in another municipality down the road it's probably not going to be that far away. Stop looking at the negative. Look for a reason to hold him close."

Harper sighed, resigned. She couldn't argue with Zander for one more second. She didn't want to. "Do you think he's a good kisser?"

Zander's handsome face split with a wide grin. "I can't wait until you find out."

. . .

"I'VE DECIDED that college boys bug me," Zander announced, casting a derisive sidelong look toward a group of male students talking near the university center entrance. "Seriously, just ... ugh."

"When we were here the other day you thought they offered a lot of potential," Harper reminded him. "What happened to change that?"

"I watched a real man come to our house with the intention of wooing you," Zander replied. "These kids don't have that potential."

"Wooing me?" Harper raised a confrontational eyebrow. "Did we slip through a time warp and into 1832?"

"You know what I mean," Zander said. "Jared was forthcoming and honest. He told you what he was thinking, he shared information, and he admitted he was still struggling with a few things. The only thing he forgot with his little visit was some flowers. I'll make sure that doesn't happen again."

"I don't even like flowers."

"Bite your tongue," Zander said. "All women should like flowers."

"That's like saying all men should like basketball."

"I like basketball."

"You do not."

"I do, too," Zander argued. "I love all the tattoos – you know I'm a sucker for tattoos – and I like all the butt patting they do."

"You're unbelievable."

"And don't you forget it," Zander said, scanning the students milling about. "What do you want to do? Are we looking for someone who slept with the professor to question them about whether or not they think he's a murderer or are we looking for possible suspects who might have hurt Annie?"

"Both."

"Well, as long as you've got your head wrapped around what we should be focused on," Zander snarked.

"I don't know what I'm looking for," Harper admitted. "I know that we need to find Annie's killer and this is the only place I know to look."

"I think you're missing the obvious answer."

"Which is?"

"Annie," Zander replied. "She knows who killed her. It's locked somewhere in her memory. Shouldn't we be focusing on her?"

"Annie may never remember," Harper said. "She doesn't want to remember. Whatever happened was traumatic enough for her to block it out. What she is seeing is coming in flashes. She doesn't want to remember being raped. It's too hard."

"I can't imagine how hard that is," Zander said, his face softening. "This is like looking for a needle in a haystack."

"That's a bad analogy," Harper countered. "It would be more like looking for a needle in a pile of other needles."

"Thank you, buzzkill."

"I don't know what else to do," Harper said. "It's not like we're missing anything at the office."

"We're missing Eric mooning over you and frothing at the mouth when he finds out you're going to start dating Jared," Zander said. "That's going to be a heck of a meltdown, by the way."

"I know," Harper said, pinching the bridge of her nose. "I don't know what to do about him. Molly was having a fit because apparently he was having a fit after Jared and I left the other day."

"Yeah, it was pretty funny," Zander chortled.

"I don't think Eric finds it funny," I said. "It was no different than Molly watching him freak out about someone else when she has a crush on him."

"I wish he would get his head out of his butt and realize she's a catch," Zander said. "I think they might be good together."

"I do, too," Harper said. "That's why I told her to date someone else."

Zander furrowed his brow. "You did? Doesn't that only exacerbate the problem?"

"I'm hoping that when Eric sees Molly with another man it makes him realize he does have feelings for her."

"He doesn't have feelings for her, hidden or otherwise, right now," Zander said. "He's too focused on you. He needs you to crush him so he can pout for a few weeks and then open himself up to moving on. He's not going to even look at Molly until that happens."

"I think you're wrong."

"Well, I know I'm right."

"I guess we'll have to agree to disagree then," Harper said.

"I think we should place a wager on it instead."

Harper clapped her hands together, taking Zander by surprise. "You're right. That sounds like more fun. Okay, how do we want to do this?"

Zander smirked. "You're feeling better about this Jared situation, aren't you?"

"What?"

"You're perking up," Zander said. "I like to see you smile. If betting makes you happy we shall bet. I say we wager fifty bucks on the fact that Eric is not going to look at Molly until you and Jared are dating."

Harper made a face. "That's a really vague bet," she said. "I'm fine with the fifty bucks. I think we need more of a time frame."

"Go on."

"I say that Eric and Molly hook up within the next six weeks," Harper said.

Zander tilted his head to the side, considering. "Sold."

They shook hands.

"Now, let's find someone to talk to so I can justify buying a really fattening coffee because I need the caffeine," Zander said.

"I . . . ."

"Well, hello again."

Harper made a face when she heard Jay's voice. It was just her luck the guy never seemed to go to class and instead spent all of his time acting like a proper jerkwad in front of the university center.

"Hello, Jay," Harper said, pasting a tight smile on her face as she swiveled to face him. "It's so nice to see you."

He apparently didn't understand sarcasm. "I knew you would be back," Jay said. "I have a certain magnetism. Women can't stay away from me."

"That's exactly why I'm here," Harper said. "I came to see you."

Jay's eyes brightened. "Really?"

"She's being sarcastic," Collin said, stepping up beside his brother and shooting Harper an apologetic look. "I'm sorry to run into you like this again."

"That makes two of us."

"Three of us," Zander corrected, narrowing his eyes as he regarded Jay as if he was something akin to a squashed bug on a windshield. "Don't you ever go to class?"

"Don't you ever dress like a normal man?" Jay asked, looking at Zander's white linen pants and pink polo shirt as if he was wearing a clown costume.

"This is a mature style," Zander said. "I know that's something you wouldn't know anything about, but it's on the pages of all the top fashion magazines."

"And in old episodes of *Miami Vice*," Harper quipped.

Zander scorched her with a look. "I thought you were on my side."

"I am on your side," Harper said, smiling at him ruefully. "You do remind me of Sonny Crockett, though."

"He was hot. You're always drooling over him when we watch reruns."

"So are you."

"Wow, you guys are really old," Jay said, rolling his eyes. "*Miami Vice*? Isn't that the movie with Collin Farrell and that guy who played the blind dude in that music movie?"

"We are definitely old," Zander muttered.

"Hey, *Miami Vice* was old when we watched it," Harper pointed out. "It's still a classic show."

"Vintage," Zander corrected.

"Vintage," Harper agreed.

"What are you guys doing back here?" Jay asked, rapidly losing interest in the pop culture conversation. "If you're not here to see me – your loss, by the way – then that means you're here to ask more questions about Annie Dresden."

"Actually, I'm looking for more information on Professor Dalton," Harper replied, an idea forming. "I know you said he made the rounds with a lot of students, but did anyone ever ... I don't know ... threaten to get him fired because of the way he dumped them?"

"There were a lot of girls who threatened him," Jay replied. "He didn't seem to care. He thinks he's untouchable."

"You don't seem to like him very much," Zander said.

"He thinks he's God's gift to women," Jay said. "The dude is old. The only reason women sleep with him is because they want to get good grades."

"Jay thinks he's God's gift to women so he doesn't like Professor Dalton because he sees him as competition," Collin explained.

"I figured that out myself," Harper said, winking at Collin.

"I *am* God's gift to women," Jay said. "Everyone wants to date me."

"Then how come you have to resort to hitting on random women on a college campus?" Jared asked, appearing out of nowhere and fixing Jay with a harsh look.

"Oh, good, the cop is back," Jay muttered. "Speaking of ... I never told the hot chick about Professor Dalton. I only told you about him. When did cops start sharing information with civilians?"

Jared shifted his eyes to Harper. "Not that I want to take this guy's side, but he has a point. How did you know exactly what he said to me that day?"

"How do you know what I know?" Harper countered.

Jared extended a finger in warning and wagged it in Harper's face. "Don't try to confuse me. How did you know?"

"Um ... ."

"Oh, just tell him so we can get our coffee," Zander said. "We were hiding in those bushes over there while you were questioning him."

Harper pursed her lips, anger with Zander warring for supremacy in her head with fear over Jared's reaction.

"I see," Jared said, smiling despite himself. "I don't know why I'm surprised. I guess that makes sense. You knew more than you were supposed to and I never questioned why. I assumed Mel told you. He tells everyone everything else."

"Wait ... you're not mad?" Harper was surprised.

"No," Jared said. "I need you to stand there and let me do my job for a second, though. Then I'm going to take you for coffee while Zander goes home."

"I want coffee," Zander whined.

"You can get coffee," Jared replied. "You just can't get it with us."

"We drove together," Harper said.

"I'll make sure you get home."

Harper nodded wordlessly, her cheeks burning under Jared's pointed gaze. Zander mimed making out with an invisible person behind Jared's back while Harper tried to ignore him.

"I know what you're doing, Zander, and if you don't stop it I'm going to thump you," Jared warned, never moving his eyes in Zander's direction.

"How did you know?"

"I can see your reflection in the window," Jared said, pointing.

"Oh, I guess that's why you're a cop," Zander said. "If you're taking over Harper duty does that mean I can go?"

"Don't you want to find out what Jared is going to ask him?" Harper protested.

"I'll wait for the highlights on CNN tonight," Zander deadpanned. "Jared, am I free to go?"

"I'm encouraging it," Jared replied.

"By, Harp." Zander kissed her cheek quickly. "I'll make enough dinner tonight for three – just in case." Zander was gleeful as he scampered away.

"He's a trip," Jared muttered.

"He's a fairy," Jay griped.

"Don't ever say that again," Jared warned, turning his hostile attention back to Jay. "I don't care if you think you're being cool or you really believe it. Show people respect for a change. You might be surprised how it benefits you."

Jared's stock was rising in Harper's estimation with every word.

"I don't want to waste a lot of time with you," Jared said. "I do want to know if you can give me the names of any of the other students Dalton slept with."

"I don't know their names," Jay said.

Jared glanced at Collin. "What about you?"

"I'm sorry," Collin said, turning his palms up as he shrugged. "I honestly don't know either. I'm not up on the gossip like Jay is. I can try to find out if you want."

"That would be great," Jared said, slipping a business card in Collin's direction. "Do me a favor and keep it quiet why you want to know."

"Will do," Collin said, nodding.

Jared held his hand out in Harper's direction, taking her by surprise for the second time in the same five-minute window. "Shall we?"

Harper eyed his hand, confused. "Shall we what?"

"It's coffee time," Jared said.

"Oh, okay."

Jared kept his hand extended. "Take my hand."

Harper did as instructed, internally sighing at the way her hand fit perfectly inside of his.

"See, that wasn't so bad," Jared said.

"You're going to make me work for every second of this, aren't you?"

"We're going to work together," Jared said. "Now, come on. We can't count this as a date, but we can enjoy our time together."

"Work, work, work."

"Sometimes the best things in life are worth the work," Jared said. "Come on."

TWENTY-TWO

"What kind of coffee do you want?" Jared asked, his fingers still linked with Harper's as he studied the menu at the university center's coffee shop.

Harper stared down at their joined hands, and when she didn't immediately answer Jared shifted his gaze over to her. "Does this bother you?"

Harper jerked her head up, surprised by the question. "No. It's just ... a few days ago you thought I was a crackpot and now ... now you're openly holding my hand."

Jared studied her for a moment. "You think I'm moving too fast. That's fair." He released Harper's hand. "Just for the record, I didn't think you were a crackpot."

Harper tilted her head to the side, shooting him a doubtful look.

"I didn't think you were a crackpot," Jared repeated. "I thought you were a scam artist."

Harper wanted to be offended, but his delectable grin was too cute to ignore. She gave in and returned the gesture. "You're funny."

"I considered being a clown before becoming a cop, but I thought it would be more fun to catch criminals than climb in a small car with ten other clowns. I'm borderline claustrophic."

Instinctively Harper reached out and grabbed his hand again, surprising herself with the gesture. "I ... um ... ."

"I can't stop touching you either," Jared said, opting for blunt honesty. "It's not like we're dropping our clothes and going for it right here. I'm perfectly fine with you holding my hand."

"I don't know why I keep doing it," Harper admitted, running her other hand through her flaxen hair.

"It's because I'm hot," Jared said. "That's what I keep telling myself when I fixate on you, too, by the way. Oh, and if you ever feel the uncontrollable urge to rip my clothes off, I'm going to be okay with that, too."

"You're good at this flirting thing," Harper said.

Jared arched an eyebrow. "Does that bother you?"

"I might be a little rusty."

Jared's face softened. "I think you're doing fine," he said. "While you and Zander don't technically flirt, that witty repartee you have going has helped keep your skills fresh."

"You're very ... understanding," Harper said, her face serious. "I thought you were the exact opposite when I first met you."

"I wasn't at my best that first day," Jared conceded. "I wasn't expecting a murder in Whisper Cove. I was trying to get to know Mel – and he's odd – and then you came along with Zander. Do you want to know what the first thing I thought when I saw you with Zander was?"

Harper nodded, intrigued.

"I hoped he was your boyfriend."

"That was *so* not what I was expecting," Harper said, wrinkling her nose. "I thought you were going to say your heart rate sped up and it felt as if you'd been hit by a bolt of lightning."

"That's exactly what I felt," Jared said. "I still wanted Zander to be your boyfriend. That would've meant you were off limits. I don't move in on other people's territory. I wasn't exactly looking to start dating someone."

"And now?"

"Now I'm pretty sure I can't keep away from you so I'm just going to go with it," Jared said. "Things may work out and they may not, but I think I'm going to drive myself crazy if I try to pretend there's nothing here.

"I don't know what's here," he continued. "I do know that ... your hand seems to fit mine. I do know that when you smile it lights up your whole face. I do know that I like listening to you talk. I also know that I'm constantly distracted by your lips."

As if on cue Harper ran her tongue over lips, drawing Jared's attention to them.

"That right there makes me want to push you against that wall and kiss you senseless," Jared said.

"You are amazingly blunt," Harper said, her breath catching.

"Don't worry. I'm not kissing you here," Jared said. "I already told you I'm not going to do that until this case is solved. I don't want death hanging over us when I make my move."

Harper snorted. "Make your move?"

"What would you call it?"

"I don't know," Harper said. She leaned forward and brazenly gave him a kiss on the cheek, taking them both by surprise.

"What was that for?" Jared asked, marveling at the warmth of her skin as it touched his. "I thought I told you we were waiting."

"You're not the boss of me," Harper said. "That's not the main event anyway. That was just a ... appetizer."

Jared grinned. "I can't wait for the entrée."

"Me either," Harper said. She took a step away from him and shook her head to snap herself out of the reverie she was mired in. "You do funny things to me. You make my stomach ... knot up."

"I know the feeling," Jared said, running his hand through his hair. "Seriously, though, what do you want to drink? If we don't turn this conversation to a safer topic I'm going to lose my head – even more than I already have."

"I'll have an iced green tea with no sweetener."

Jared made a face. "That sounds ... healthy."

"I'm addicted to green tea," Harper said, her expression rueful. "I used to be addicted to Diet Coke, but Zander broke me of that habit when he bought the Keurig."

"Green tea it is," Jared said, bringing their joined hands up and brushing a quick kiss across her knuckles. "Why don't you go and get straws and napkins and find us a table?"

Harper nodded. "Okay."

Their eyes were still locked on one another and Jared knew that any outsider looking in would see the sexual tension oozing between them. He reluctantly let her hand go. "Find a table away from everyone else if you can."

"Are you sure that's a good idea?" Harper teased. "What if I get an overwhelming urge to rip your clothes off?"

"That's what I'm hoping for," Jared said, reaching up and running his thumb down her smooth cheek. "I'll find you in a few minutes."

"I'm looking forward to it."

HARPER WAS HAVING trouble putting words to the feelings cascading through her. She hadn't felt anything like this since Quinn. No, that wasn't true. She'd been genuinely fond of Quinn. He was comfortable, attractive, and fun. He'd never shaken her to the core like Jared did with a simple look, though.

Part of Harper felt guilty for that realization. She knew Quinn wasn't her soul mate – and she believed in soul mates, especially now – but she was starting to think she'd only been going through the motions with him. Jared was something different.

She was so lost in thought she didn't notice the figure moving in behind her until Molly was practically upon her. "Harper!"

Harper jumped, clutching the napkins closer to her chest as she swiveled. Molly's face was a mixture of excitement and glee and Harper couldn't help but smile at the young woman's enthusiasm. "What's up?"

"I saw you come in here with the hot cop," Molly said. "Where is he?"

"Ordering drinks."

LILY HARPER HART

"You were holding his hand," Molly said, her ski-slope nose wrinkling. "You said you weren't interested in him."

"I was probably lying to you and myself," Harper admitted. "I'm definitely interested in him."

Molly squealed and grabbed Harper's hand. "That's so great. I'm so happy for you."

"We're having coffee, not getting married," Harper said, refusing to give in to her inner urges and squeal right along with Molly. "We're just getting to know one another."

"I'm still happy for you," Molly said. "You deserve someone to … have coffee with."

Harper snorted. "It does sound nice," she said. "What are you doing here?"

"I finished up my last exam," Molly said. "I'm all yours for the summer."

"Speaking of that, Zander and I have been talking," Harper said. "We're going to start paying you, especially since you're going to be working full time this summer. Summer is a busy time for us and we think you deserve a little something thanks to all the hard work you do."

"But … I volunteered as an intern. You don't have to pay me. I love working with you guys."

"I know you do," Harper said. "You also work hard and when you work hard you deserve to get paid for it. You've been with us a long time now, Molly. You're part of our family."

"I'm so excited." Molly threw her arms around Harper's neck and drew her in for a tight hug.

"Did I miss something?" Jared asked, a drink in each hand as he rounded the corner and caught sight of Molly and Harper.

Harper disengaged herself from the boisterous college student. "Jared, this is Molly. She's been an intern with us for … wow, thirteen months now … and I just told her she was going to get paid for her work this summer."

"Ah," Jared said, handing Harper her green tea while eyeing Molly. "Are you telling me you were a slave driver before this?"

"No," Harper said, making a face.

"I volunteered," Molly explained. "I heard about them on campus and I went out to their office and I fell in love with Harper and Zander the moment I met them. This only proves I was right."

"Harper and Zander should have their own sitcom," Jared agreed, although his smile was genuine as he gazed at Molly. "What are you going to school for?"

"Liberal arts."

Jared made a face. "What kind of job are you going to get with that?"

"The same kind of job I have now," Molly said. "Once I graduate in a year I'm going to take over marketing of GHI and I'm going to take us statewide ... and then nationwide ... and then worldwide."

Jared pursed his lips and cast a sidelong look in Harper's direction. "Are you going worldwide?"

"I'm going to settle for making it out of St. Clair, Macomb, and Oakland counties right now."

"Good to know," Jared said. He turned his attention back to Molly. "Not that I'm not happy for you, and you obviously deserve your big break, but we were going to have some coffee and talk."

Molly nodded happily. "I know. I saw you come inside together. Holding hands, I might add."

Jared refused to be embarrassed by Molly's pointed comment. "She has nice hands."

"I've seen her change when we go clothes shopping, too," Molly said. "You're not going to be disappointed when you get to see that either."

Jared's chuckle was warm and hearty. "I'm betting you're right," he said.

Harper's cheeks were burning and she focused on the green tea in her hand because she was afraid to meet Jared and Molly's mischievous eyes. "I can't believe I'm in the middle of this conversation."

"Me either," Jared said. "I thought we would be in the middle of a completely different uncomfortable conversation between just the two of us by now."

"I got your hint the first time," Molly said, shooting him a look. "I'm not trying to third-wheel your date. I have a date of my own, in fact."

"You do?" Harper lifted her eyebrows and focused on Molly. "When did this happen?"

"I took your advice," Molly said. "Eric is never going to notice I'm alive as long as I'm too available for him. He's too in love with you to even recognize me when we're in the same room together."

"Who is Eric?" Jared asked, his interest piqued.

"He's the other guy who works out of our office," Harper replied.

"The one with the dark hair and leather coat?"

Harper nodded.

"He's in love with you?" Jared asked.

"No," Harper said, waving off the question as if it were nothing more than a pesky fly. "He has a crush on me."

"And you have a crush on him?" Jared asked Molly.

"I guess, although I don't like the word 'crush,'" Molly said. "I find him interesting and would like to see what he looks like naked."

Jared bit his bottom lip as his gaze bounced between the two women. "I see," he said finally. "You don't like him, though, right?"

Harper didn't get a chance to answer because Molly did it for her. "Harper is always nice to Eric, but she isn't sexually attracted to him," she said. "In fact, I wasn't sure if she was ever going to be sexually attracted to anyone until you came along. I'm so relieved to find out her hormones actually work."

"I am, too," Jared said, grinning. "For curiosity's sake, though, what advice did Harper give you to make Eric realize you were alive?"

"She told me to date someone else to make Eric jealous." Molly's answer was simple, but it set off a firestorm in Jared's head.

"How come you didn't try to make me jealous?" Jared asked pointedly.

"Because you already knew I was alive," Harper replied, not missing a beat.

"I guess that's true," Jared said, using his free hand to rub his stubbled jaw. "It's hard to pretend you're not alive when you're so ... pretty."

"Oh, he's so sweet," Molly said, pressing her hand to her heart. "He's hot and charming. It's like you're a unicorn."

Jared arched an eyebrow. "Excuse me?"

"Unicorns are mythical and magical beasts that are coveted by all," Molly explained. "You're a unicorn."

"I have no idea how to take that," Jared admitted.

"It's a compliment."

"It is," Harper agreed, turning back to Molly. "Who are you going out with?"

"You told me to ask Collin out, so I did," Molly said.

"I used Collin as an example of a nice guy who might be interested in you," Harper clarified. "I didn't suggest that you go and ask him out right away."

"Well, I did and he agreed," Molly said. "We're going to a house party to celebrate the end of finals tonight."

"That sounds fun," Harper said. "I just saw Collin with his brother out on the front lawn."

Molly perked up. "You did? How did he look?"

"Um ... handsome?" Harper looked to Jared for support. "You would say Collin looked handsome, wouldn't you?"

"Which one is Collin?" Jared asked.

"Jay's brother. The one you gave your business card to."

Jared scowled. "I don't mind that kid, but his brother should be locked up for being a douche."

"I think we'd all like to see that," Harper agreed.

"Jay has a reputation as a minute man on campus," Molly said. "I wouldn't worry about it. He'll be appreciated for the loser he is as soon as his looks go."

"A minute man?" Harper asked, confused.

"Yeah, as in he lasts for a minute ... and I'm being generous," Molly said. "I don't personally know that for a fact, but I know two girls who told me. He's a three-stroke maniac."

"Oh, my." Harper's hand flew up to her mouth as she tried to keep from laughing out loud.

Jared didn't bother hiding his mirth. "That doesn't surprise me about Jay. Have fun on your date with his brother."

It was a pointed dismissal, but it caused Molly to roll her eyes instead of immediately leaving. "I do have one question, Harper," she said. "Don't worry, Mr. Cop, it won't take long and then you can continue your ... hand-holding date."

"Thank you, Miss Molly," Jared replied, unruffled. "Ask your question quickly because I have limited time before I have to be back at the office and you're eating it all up."

"How much can I tell Collin about what we do?" Molly asked. "I've never really talked to anyone about my job at GHI unless I know them really well. Is it okay if I tell Collin we put ghosts to rest?"

"That's up to you," Harper said. "I'm not ashamed of what we do. I've found that it's probably better to tell people sooner rather than later, though."

"Why?"

"You don't want to get attached to someone and then find out they're not going to accept the ghost thing," Harper said, casting a furtive look in Jared's direction. He saw the look but didn't comment on it.

"That's a good point," Molly said. "I'll tell him. If he's flaky I'll only keep him around for two more dates so Eric can see us together and get really jealous."

"Good idea."

Molly gave Harper one more quick hug and then disappeared. By the time it was just the two of them their drinks were mostly gone.

"I'm sorry she monopolized our ... coffee thing," Harper said.

"It's okay," Jared replied. "I'm glad she showed up. She's a fount of interesting gossip. I now know Eric is in love with you and I might have to pound him at some point, and I also know you're worried I'm not going to accept the ghost thing."

"I ... how did you know that?" Harper was flabbergasted.

"I saw the look on your face," Jared said. "It's okay. I already accept the ghost thing."

"But ... how?"

"I believe in you," Jared replied, guileless. "I don't know why. I don't know how. I just know I do. I won't walk away because of the ghost stuff."

"What will you walk away for?"

"Right now? Nothing," Jared replied. "I can't make promises about what's going to happen next week ... or next month ... or next year. All I can promise is I want to get to know you and learn more about what you do."

"I guess that's a pretty good answer," Harper said, sipping her green tea.

"It's the only one I have," Jared said.

"If it's any consolation I'm very excited to see you naked someday, too." Harper had no idea where the flirtatious words came from, but she wasn't sorry she uttered them when she saw Jared's cheeks flush with color for a change.

"That's definitely something to look forward to," he said.

TWENTY-THREE

"How was your date with Officer Hottie?" Zander asked, handing Harper a glass of iced tea and settling on the couch next to her later that evening.

"It wasn't technically a date."

"I heard you were holding hands," Zander challenged.

"Molly has a huge mouth," Harper muttered.

"She called to thank me for paying her this summer," Zander said. "I thought we were going to tell her together."

"I'm sorry," Harper said, instantly contrite. "I know we were going to do it together, but she was there ... and I was nervous ... and it fit into the conversation. I shouldn't have told her."

"It's fine," Zander said. "As much as I like to imagine she's hung around GHI for the past year without pay because of my sparkling personality, I really know it's because she's infatuated with you."

"She's infatuated with Eric," Harper corrected.

"She has a crush on Eric," Zander agreed. "You're her mentor, though."

"Mentor?" Harper made a face as she comically lifted an eyebrow.

"Scoff if you will ... ."

"All right," Harper said. "No one is looking at me as a mentor. Trust me. No one wants to be me."

"You're my hero," Zander said. "I want to be you. Well ... I don't want to dress like you. You should wear heels instead of sneakers some days. They would make your legs look longer, and you have great legs. You also wear an appalling amount of polyester and I wish you would embrace some more color into your wardrobe."

"How did this turn into an episode of *America's Next Top Model*?"

Zander ignored her. "You're also brave, loyal, true, sweet, funny, and you have a huge heart," he said. "On the flip side, when I need you to be, you're catty, mean and gossipy. You're the perfect package.

"I don't think you should be wondering who would want to be you," he continued. "The question is: Who wouldn't want to be you?"

Harper blinked rapidly to fight off a sudden burst of tears. Zander always knew the right thing to say. He also knew the wrong thing to say, but that wasn't the case at this precise moment. "You're the best friend I'm ever going to have."

"Don't you dare cry," Zander said, waving a finger in her face. "You're the best friend I'm ever going to have. I would still think you're a pretty great mentor even if you weren't my best friend."

"You're the best ego booster ever," Harper said, leaning over and giving him a kiss on the cheek. Instead of pulling back, though, she rested her head on his shoulder. "Thank you for being in my life."

"I can't live without you," Zander replied, tugging on his never-ending supply of false bravado. "You don't have to thank me. I would literally die without you."

"You're a trip."

"You're a trip."

"What do you want to watch tonight?" Harper asked, turning the conversation to a topic that wouldn't threaten either of their tear ducts.

"How about some *Modern Family* reruns?"

"Sold."

. . .

"**HOW** was your coffee date with Harper?" Mel asked, sliding a sly look in the direction of Jared's desk.

Jared didn't bother looking up from the file he was perusing. "Nice. I would've preferred some more time alone with her, but we had a good time."

Mel shifted in his chair, surprised. "Aren't you going to ask how I knew about your coffee date?"

"Zander knew about it so I don't have to ask."

"You're already getting used to us gossiping about you," Mel mused. "That's a good sign."

"I don't care how much you gossip."

"You just care about Harper," Mel teased.

"She's an interesting woman," Jared agreed, furrowing his brow as he studied the file in his hand.

"What are you looking at?"

"We got a few tips over the phone," Jared said. "The secretary wrote them down, but I'm not sure anyone bothered to look at them. I want to make sure we're not missing something on the Annie Dresden case."

"What do you think we might be missing?"

"I don't know," Jared said. "I ... something feels off."

"I think it's the professor," Mel said. "He had motive and means. He doesn't have an alibi for the night she died."

"That's not true. I do have an alibi."

Jared jerked at the sound of Professor Dalton's voice, glancing up to find him standing in the doorway of the office with his lawyer, Peter Barnett, at his side.

"What are you doing here?" Jared asked. "I thought you were done talking to us. Isn't that what you said?"

"It is," Dalton conceded. "It's just ... ." He exchanged a look with his attorney.

"My client and I have talked about this at length," Barnett said. "I'm not keen on him sharing information with you, but I'm also not keen on having this go any further than it has to. My client is innocent ... and he can prove it."

"We're all ears," Jared said, gesturing toward the chairs on the other side of his desk.

"IT'S A NICE NIGHT," Molly said, giggling as she settled in one of the lawn chairs outside the big colonial house and fixed Collin with a coquettish look. "Spring is finally here and you can tell summer is right around the corner."

"You can," Collin agreed, taking the spot next to her and sipping his beer. "I love this time of year."

"Me, too," Molly enthused. "Summer is my favorite time, but I love spring – and even fall to some extent, as well."

"I guess that means you hate winter," Collin teased, winking.

"Doesn't everyone hate a Michigan winter?"

"I don't," Jay said, appearing out of nowhere and plopping down in one of the other chairs on the patio.

Collin scowled at his brother. "What are you doing out here? I thought you found a woman inside that you were going to bother all night."

"She disappeared," Jay said, shrugging. "I think I was too much for her. I need a woman with more substance. I think this one will do nicely." He patted Molly's knee suggestively. "You're kind of cute. Those pink streaks in your hair are distracting, but once we're in bed I'll bet I hardly notice."

Molly made a face. "I wouldn't sleep with you if you were the last man on Earth and I only had thirty seconds to live," she said. "By the way, that's what I hear you're good for ... thirty seconds."

Jay's version of a "come hither" looked shifted into a "go away" look pretty quickly by Molly's estimation – and she was pleased to see him deflate, if only a little.

"I don't need your crap," Jay snapped. "I know you're trying to pretend you're interested in my brother, but I'm here to tell you no one believes it."

"I *am* interested in your brother," Molly replied, not missing a beat. "Even if I wasn't, though, I wouldn't be interested in you."

"Whatever," Jay said, rolling his eyes until they landed on Collin. "This party sucks. We should try to find another one that doesn't have such frigid girls."

Molly's heart dropped at the suggestion. While she and Collin were still getting to know one another, she was looking forward to the process. While she was still more interested in hanging around Collin to make Eric jealous than anything else, she also found him to be articulate and thoughtful and she was starting to realize he might be an actual contender in the romance game. If he left with Jay, that would all end. "You're going?"

Collin shot her an apologetic look. "I'm not going," he said. "I'm ... sorry ... about him. He always does this."

"I don't want to stay here," Jay whined.

"Then go," Collin suggested.

"I have plans for this evening," Jay growled.

"No one is standing in your way," Collin countered.

"That's not true. You're standing in my way."

Collin got to his feet wearily. "Do you mind waiting here for a few minutes while I walk my brother back to his car?"

"No," Molly replied, internally sighing with relief because Collin was opting to remove his brother from their date. "I'll be right here."

"Great."

"I MIGHT HAVE LIED when I said I didn't have an alibi," Dalton said, shifting in his chair uncomfortably as he met Jared's serious gaze. "I ... was with someone the night Annie was killed."

"Another student?" Jared asked, fighting to tamp down his disgust.

"That's just it ... um ... I would have proudly told you if I was with a student," Dalton said. "I've been seeing someone else for about a week now and I don't want it to get out."

Jared was confused. "I'm not sure what that means."

"Please tell me you're not dating a high school student," Mel said, pinching the bridge of his nose. "You know we have to arrest you if your alibi is an underage girl, right?"

GHOSTLY INTERESTS

"That's not it," Dalton said. "I ... it's actually an overage girl."

Jared furrowed his brow. "Excuse me?"

"I've been dating the librarian at the school," Dalton blurted out, covering his eyes as shame washed over him.

Jared shifted his attention to Bennett. "Do you want to explain this without all the theatrics?"

"Trista Nelson is the librarian at St. Clair Community College," Bennett explained. "She and Professor Dalton have a sexual relationship."

"Why is that such a big deal?" Mel queried.

"She's thirty," Bennett replied.

"And that's a problem?" Jared asked.

"She's thirty," Dalton hissed. "If people find out I'm sleeping with someone my own age my reputation will take a huge hit."

Jared swallowed the mad urge to laugh. "I see. I thought you were thirty-five?"

"I am."

"Then this librarian would still be younger than you," Jared pointed out.

"She's still old," Dalton complained.

"I know I'm going to regret asking this but ... if you think she's too old, why are you sleeping with her?" Jared asked.

"Because it's nice to have someone who knows what they're doing in bed for a change," Dalton said. "I like being a teacher, but sometimes I like being schooled."

Jared and Mel exchanged twin grimaces.

"Okay," Jared said, shaking his head. "I'm assuming you were with Trista the night Annie was killed. For how long?"

"The whole night," Dalton said. "She's a stickler for no pump and dumps. She demands my attention for the entire evening."

Jared wanted to laugh. The situation was so surreal it was almost dumbfounding. "Why didn't you just tell us this from the beginning?"

"I already told you that I don't want it getting out that I'm dating an older woman," Dalton replied.

"Why are you telling us now?"

"My client is worried that you're zeroing in on him as a suspect," Bennett said. "I wanted to address the situation before it got out of hand. Personally, I don't see the problem dating a thirty-year-old woman. My client sees it another way. It's not for me to judge.

"Regardless, my client didn't rape and kill Annie Dresden," he continued. "You're looking in the wrong direction."

"We're going to have to contact Ms. Nelson to verify this," Mel warned.

"I know." Dalton looked miserable.

"For the sake of argument, say I believe you," Jared said. "You still have motive. Annie was threatening to show those photographs of the two of you in bed to the dean."

"It's not the first time," Dalton said. "Three different girls showed photos to the dean. He doesn't like it, but I'm popular. I'm not going to get fired over it. Besides, I look good in those photos. If Annie spread them around I would've had even more women after me."

Jared couldn't argue with the man's ego. "You knew Annie," he said. "Can you think of anyone else who would have a grudge, or reason to hurt her, besides yourself?"

"Just one person."

Jared leaned forward. "Who?"

"I'M SORRY ABOUT JAY," Collin said, returning to his spot next to Molly a few minutes later. "He's ... difficult."

"I have a sister who is the same way," Molly said sympathetically. "She goes out of her way to get attention. She doesn't care if it's negative attention. She wants it any way she can get it. Jay reminds me of her."

"That sounds about right," Collin said. "He's so frustrating."

"Is he older than you or are you older than him?"

"We're fraternal twins," Collin replied.

Molly stilled, surprised. "Really?"

"I know," Collin said, making a face. "He's taller than I am. He's blond and I have brown hair. He's better looking than I am. No one would ever guess we're twins."

"It's not that," Molly said. "I ... you're also nicer than him. I don't care what you say, though, you're attractive. You don't look alike, but you're still attractive."

"That's nice of you to say," Collin said. "I'm aware of my lot in life, though. I know Jay is better looking than I am."

"I guess it's good that you're smarter then," Molly said, winking at Collin.

"Definitely," Collin chuckled. "So, Molly, I feel like our date got interrupted at the worst time. Tell me a little bit about yourself."

"Well, I have one year left on a liberal arts degree and I also work for GHI out in Whisper Cove."

"What's GHI?"

"Ghost Hunters, Inc.," Molly said, opting to tell the truth. She liked Collin. She could only hope he had an open mind. If he didn't, it was better to find out now.

"Ghost Hunters, Inc. As in ... ghosts?" Collin's eyes widened, surprise washing over him. "I ... wow. Please don't think I'm making fun of you but ... um ... do you believe in ghosts?"

"I do," Molly said.

"Have you ever seen one?"

"Only special people can see them with the naked eye," Molly explained. "We have special equipment, though. There are air ion counters because ghosts give off electromagnetic charges, EMF detectors, EVP devices, hydrometers, infrared and thermal scanners, thermal imaging scopes, thermometers ... you name it."

"Wow, that sounds scientific," Collin said, his interest evident. "What kind of things have you seen?"

"I've seen objects flying through the air," Molly said. "I wish I could see and talk to ghosts like Harper, but I can't."

Collin shifted in his seat. "Harper is the blond woman, right?"

Molly nodded.

"She can see and talk to ghosts? How does that work?"

"I'm not really sure how it works," Molly said. "I know she's been able to do it since she was a kid. Sometimes we get hired for jobs and she can talk ghosts over to the other side. Other times the ghosts are more ... active and angry ... and we have to trap them and force them over to the other side."

"That is ... wow. That sounds exciting."

"It is," Molly said. "I love it. After I graduate I want to join the company full time. I think I can get us clients all over the world. Harper and Zander stick close to home now, but I want to change that."

"I can't believe I've met someone who talks to ghosts," Collin mused. "That's pretty interesting."

"It's definitely interesting," Molly agreed. "Right now we're working on Annie Dresden's case. We're not getting paid for it, but when Harper ran across her ghost on the beach she got drawn in. We're hoping to solve her murder in the next couple of days."

"Annie Dresden is a ghost?" Collin asked. "I ... and Harper has been talking to her?"

Molly's head bobbed up and down enthusiastically.

"Did Annie say what happened to her?"

"She doesn't remember all of it," Molly said. "It's traumatic for new ghosts. She remembers leaving the library and she told Harper about her iPad so we know that's missing."

"Will she ever remember?"

"Most likely," Molly said. "We just have to wait so she can tell Harper and then Harper can tell Jared."

"And Jared is the cop?" Collin asked.

"Yes."

"Wow. I'm ... stunned," Collin said, his face unreadable. He reached over and snagged Molly's glass. "I'm going to get a refill. I'll get one for you, too, and then we can talk more about this. I find it ... fascinating."

"That sounds great," Molly said. "By the way, Collin, I don't care what you think. You're very handsome and charming. Your brother has nothing on you."

"Thank you," Collin said. "I'm glad someone finally noticed."

TWENTY-FOUR

"Do you want popcorn?" Zander asked.

"I'm too comfortable to move," Harper replied, her head still resting against his shoulder.

"I can make it."

"If you move I'll have to move."

Zander sighed. "Do you always have to be this difficult?"

Harper matched his dramatic sigh. "Shouldn't you have prefaced your initial question by saying that you wanted popcorn and you were willing to share it with me?"

"I will for future reference," Zander said. He gave Harper a quick kiss on the forehead and then pushed himself up from the couch. "Do you want parmesan or cheddar cheese sprinkled on the popcorn?"

"What do you want?"

"Parmesan."

"That's fine," Harper said, her gaze trained on the television. "Have you ever considered that we're kind of like Mitch and Claire on *Modern Family*?"

"Wow, it's nice out here in left field," Zander teased. "What made you think of that?"

"I don't know," Harper said, shrugging. "You just remind me of Mitch."

"Are you saying I'm fussy?"

"No more than I am."

"Well, at least you're still treating us as if we're equals," Zander said. He shuffled into the kitchen and Harper could hear him rummaging around for popcorn and a bowl. "Hey, did you leave the back door open?"

"Yes. I often enjoy leaving the door open so strangers can walk in and bugs can fly around our house."

Zander didn't immediately respond.

"Zander? You're supposed to give me a witty comeback."

Harper was met with nothing but silence so she leaned forward to get a clearer view of the kitchen. Zander was nowhere in sight. "Zander?"

A hint of movement caught her attention and Harper released a pent-up sigh of relief. She didn't even realize she'd been holding her breath until it came whooshing out.

"Aren't you going to answer me?" Harper asked.

"That's not Zander," Annie whispered, popping into view.

Harper jumped at her sudden arrival. "It's not? Who is it? It's probably my dad. Don't worry about it."

"It's not your dad," Annie said, her voice low. "He's here."

"YOU KNOW someone who wanted to hurt Annie Dresden?" Jared asked, surprised.

Dalton nodded. "Actually I do. I know you want to believe that Annie was this good girl who got done wrong, but she had more enemies than you might suspect."

"Tell me," Jared said, leaning back in his chair and clasping his hands behind his head.

"She was a slut."

Mel scorched Dalton with a look. "Is that really necessary?"

"I'm sorry," Dalton said, holding his hands up. "She was, though. I wasn't the only professor she slept with, and she made her way through quite an impressive chunk of the student population."

"Meaning?"

"She was constantly trying to find a boyfriend in an environment where no one wants to have a girlfriend," Dalton said. "College boys don't want relationships that last forever. They want easy access to … lady parts. A college campus is not where you find a forever mate and yet that's exactly what Annie was looking for."

"You're saying Annie was looking for someone to love her and she kept running into men who only wanted to have sex with her," Jared said.

Dalton nodded. "I know of at least three guys she semi-stalked on campus after they had sex with her and dumped her."

"Did she go after them with photos like she went after you?"

"I can't answer that," Dalton said. "All I know is that Annie liked to take photos in bed and I doubt I'm the only one she was doing it with."

"Who are these other guys?"

"Michael Sampson, for one. I think Danny Dwyer was another. Oh, and Jay Graham."

Jared leaned forward, his eyes keen. "Jay Graham? Annie had sex with Jay Graham? Are you sure?"

"I'm sure," Dalton said. "They had a big blow up outside of class one day because he promised to call and he didn't."

Mel and Jared exchanged a look.

"What are you thinking?" Mel asked.

"Jay Graham denied knowing Annie other than to see her on campus or say hello in passing," Jared said. "In fact, he admitted asking her out but he told me she refused. Why would he do that?"

"Maybe he was afraid to admit they had sex because he didn't want to be a suspect."

"Or maybe he was covering his tracks," Jared said. "How did Jay react to Annie's scene?"

"He seemed to like it," Dalton said. "His brother was embarrassed for both of them. I think he was mad because he had a crush on Annie.

Jay gets off on the attention, though. He thinks we're in a competition for girls, but we're really not."

"I haven't liked that kid from the start," Jared admitted.

"That doesn't mean he's a murderer," Mel pointed out.

"It doesn't. How do you know Collin liked Annie? He made like he barely knew her, too."

"I paired everyone up for a project and Collin approached me and asked to be paired with Annie," Dalton said. "I didn't see the harm in it, and I was hopeful that Annie would get off my back if someone else paid attention to her, so I paired them up."

"Instead of showing interest in Collin, though, she turned her attention to Jay, right?"

Dalton nodded.

Jared got to his feet and started pacing. Things were slipping into place, but he had two suspects and not enough motive. "Did Collin take the news that Jay and Annie slept together hard?"

"I'm a professor," Dalton said. "I'm not their friend. I hear about some of the gossip, but I can't see into their hearts. I have no idea if he was crushed or if he was okay with it. Collin has never been any trouble. He's the exact opposite of his brother."

"It has to be hard to have a douche like that as your older brother," Jared agreed.

"Jay isn't older than Collin. They're twins."

Jared stilled. "What? Jay looks older, though. Collin still looks like a kid."

"That doesn't change the fact that they're twins," Dalton said, nonplussed. "I was surprised, too."

"Okay, I need the contact information for Trista," Jared said. "You're not officially cleared, but if this checks out you can breathe a little easier."

"Oh, well, that's a relief," Dalton said, sarcasm practically dripping from his tongue. "I'm not a murder suspect but I am the guy sleeping with an older woman and I just know everyone is going to find out about it."

"Have you ever considered that dating an older woman probably saved you in this case?" Jared asked.

"I . . . ." Dalton was at a loss for words.

"I'm taking that as a no," Jared said. "Here's the thing: You dated someone in your own age bracket and the universe rewarded you. You might want to take that as a sign."

"A sign of what? That I have to date older women for the rest of my life?" Dalton was disgusted. "My life is over."

"Yeah, well, I can't help you there," Jared said. "How about you get out of our office and take that whole ... dumbass thing you've got going for yourself and bug someone else with it?"

"What are you going to do?" Dalton asked. "Are you going to arrest Jay and Collin?"

"I don't have evidence against either of them," Jared replied.

"I don't think it's going to hurt to go and talk to them again tomorrow, though," Mel added.

"Yeah, we're definitely doing that," Jared said. "For tonight, though, we're at a standstill. Have a good night."

"With your old girlfriend," Mel added, poking Dalton merely because he could.

"I knew this was going to come back and bite me," Dalton grumbled.

"WHO IS IT?" Harper asked, fear bubbling up in her chest even though she had no idea who was in the kitchen.

"I was on campus," Annie said, her voice flat. "I was looking around. I went to the library, hoping it would jog my memory. It didn't. I went to the university center and I didn't remember anything. I was walking down one of those streets on the west side of campus and that's when I saw him. I saw him and I remembered. I remembered everything."

"Who?" Harper repeated. She took a small step forward, her eyes trained on the kitchen. She couldn't see or hear Zander. She didn't take that as a good sign. He said the back door was open and then ... nothing.

"You have to run," Annie said. "He'll kill you."

"I'm not leaving Zander."

"He's probably already dead," Annie spat.

Harper's heart rolled painfully and she momentarily pressed her eyes shut. When she opened them again she was determined. "Tell me who is in that room."

"Probably not the person you're expecting," Collin said, moving into the doorframe that separated the living room and kitchen. "Hello, Harper."

Harper swallowed hard, focusing on maintaining her breathing in an even pattern so Collin couldn't detect how frightened she was. "You? You killed Annie?"

"Isn't that what your ghostly friend just told you?" Collin asked, his brown eyes glowing with malevolence as he glanced around the living room. "Are you the only one here?"

"Where is Zander?"

"The gay guy? He's in the kitchen. He's taking a nap."

That wasn't the answer Harper was looking for. "Did you kill him?"

"Not yet," Collin said. "I will before I leave here tonight, but you're my worry right now. Zander is taking a nap. He won't wake up from it, though. I can promise you that."

Harper's blood ran cold. The amiable boy she met on campus days before was gone. She didn't know who had taken up residence in his body, but this man was ... evil. She didn't know how she missed it. "Why did you kill Annie?"

"Isn't she here with us?" Collin asked. "Why not ask her? I'm just dying to know if this ghost thing is for real or not."

"Ghost thing," Harper said, half talking to herself. "You know I can talk to ghosts. Molly told you that, didn't she?"

"Molly is a talkative girl," Collin said, chuckling. "Well, Molly *was* a talkative girl."

"Did you kill Molly?" Harper choked on the words.

"Molly is in a better place," Collin said. "Of course, Annie was supposed to be in a better place, too. Imagine my surprise when little Molly told me she was still hanging around tonight."

Harper licked her lips, her heart beating so hard she was having trouble focusing. Somehow she had to get control of this situation. She had no idea where to start. "Why did you kill Annie?" she repeated.

"Ask Annie," Collin prodded.

Harper looked him up and down. With the bright light of the kitchen illuminating his frame he looked bigger than she remembered. She scanned his body, searching for a weapon, but she didn't see anything that would suggest he was armed.

"Ask Annie," Collin repeated, grotesquely contorting his face.

"Why did Collin kill you?" Harper asked, keeping her gaze on Collin as she asked the question of Annie.

"Because I slept with Jay," Annie replied.

"You slept with Jay?' Harper wrinkled her nose in disgust.

"She told you she slept with Jay?" Collin was intrigued. "Ask her why she did it?"

"She can hear you," Harper explained.

"I thought Jay was interested in me," Annie said. "I … just wanted someone to love me."

"And you thought Jay was going to love you?" Harper asked. "The guy is a raging hormone and jackass. How could you have possibly thought he was going to love you?"

"After Professor Dalton … ."

"Another great choice," Harper muttered.

"After him I felt low," Annie said. "I was sad. I thought for sure I would be the one to make him fall in love with me. I don't know how I was so wrong."

"That still doesn't explain why you thought Jay would love you," Harper said.

"What is she saying?" Collin asked.

Harper held up her finger to still him. Even as she listened to Annie she was trying to formulate a plan. She had to get to Zander.

She wouldn't leave him. That meant she had to get her hands on a weapon to fight off Collin. She needed time to think.

"I didn't think Jay would love me," Annie said. "Not really. I thought ... I don't know ... maybe he wasn't as bad as everyone kept saying."

Harper relayed Annie's comments to Collin, causing him to scowl.

"The problem with that is I really liked Annie," Collin said. "I went to Dalton and asked to be paired with her for a project. I knew he would go for it because he was embarrassed about her causing scenes and threatening him. I was going to make her forget about Dalton."

"I didn't know," Annie said.

"Did Jay know you liked Annie?" Harper asked.

"Of course he knew," Collin spat. "He always slept with the women I liked. I tried to keep it a secret, but he overheard me talking to Dalton. He made it his mission to go after Annie then.

"He went out of his way to shower her with attention," he continued. "He met her before class and he walked her to her car after class. He didn't even like her. He barely thought she was pretty. He only slept with her because I wanted her."

"Why didn't you ask him to stop?" Harper asked.

"Ask him to stop? My brother gets off on the misery of others. That would've been the same as cutting my balls off and handing them to him on a silver platter."

That was a horrific visual. Harper swallowed hard. "He's your brother. Surely he cares about you."

"Jay only cares about himself," Collin shot back. "He wants to win. He wants everything in his life to go right and everything in my life to go wrong."

Harper wanted to argue with the sentiment, but she knew it was a waste of time. Jay had no redeeming qualities. "I'm guessing he lorded it over you when he finally slept with Annie."

"He did," Collin agreed. "Apparently they took photos of themselves in bed. Jay showed them to me."

"Oh, no," Annie said, her ghostly hands flying up to her face.

"You took a lot of photos," Harper said to Annie. "That was stupid."

"I wanted proof that someone loved me," Annie wailed.

"Except you picked people who could never love you," Harper pointed out. She was starting to think Annie was just as broken as the people she was most attracted to. "If you were so upset with what Jay did, why did you go after Annie instead of him, Collin?"

"Because he's my brother and I would be a suspect in his death," Collin replied. "Everyone knows I hate him. Even if they didn't know it right away, killing Jay would only cause grief for my family. Killing Annie made me feel better."

"You stole her iPad because you wanted the photos, didn't you?" Harper asked.

"I stole the iPad because I wanted all evidence of Annie's relationship with my brother destroyed," Collin countered. "I knew the cops would come to campus looking for suspects. With the iPad destroyed there would be no link to Jay."

"Therefore there would be no link to you," Harper finished.

"Exactly."

"You thought you were in the clear until Molly told you about GHI and Annie, didn't you?"

"I honestly did," Collin said. "I thought the cops would either pin it on Dalton or eventually let it go. The semester is over. I won't be returning to the campus until the fall. I was free and clear ... until you."

"I won't tell anyone," Harper said. "I ... Zander won't either. You can go and I promise I won't say anything."

"We both know that's a lie," Collin said. "Molly told me all about how loyal and true you are. You wouldn't cover up a murder. Stop saying you would."

"I would do anything to protect the people I love," Harper argued. "I love Zander more than anyone else in the world."

"I guess it's a good thing you're dying with him then."

TWENTY-FIVE

Jared and Mel said their goodbyes at the police station door, both agreeing to meet up early the next morning to form their plan of attack. Jared was more convinced than ever that Collin or Jay was the guilty party. Now he just had to figure out which one was the culprit – and why.

While Jay was the easiest suspect, he didn't appear to have a clear motive. He wouldn't have cared if Annie spread it around campus that they slept together and he dumped her. Everyone already knew that was how he operated.

Collin was harder to fit into the mold of a killer and yet that was the direction Jared was leaning. The young man was overshadowed by a better-looking brother and often overlooked by the opposite sex. If he convinced himself that he belonged with Annie and then she rebuffed him for his brother ... that could be motivation for an already fragile mind.

As he was pulling out of the police station parking lot Jared initially turned right so he could head toward his house. He'd only gone a few blocks when he changed his mind and turned in the opposite direction – the one that led to Harper's house.

He was feeling that urge again. He wanted to see Harper. He couldn't explain it and he didn't want to fight it.

An hour hanging out with her and Zander couldn't hurt anything. Maybe he could even get that kiss he'd been dreaming about.

"I CAN'T BELIEVE you're the kind of person who would kill innocent people," Harper said, her hands shaking as she rubbed them against her hips. Her fingers were numb and she was worried, thanks to her overwhelming fear, that she was going to pass out. If she did, both she and Zander were done for. She knew that. She had to stay focused if she wanted to save them both.

"Well, believe it," Collin said, rolling his eyes. "My therapist says I'm a sociopath. I didn't believe him until now. The idea of killing you doesn't upset me. In fact, I kind of want to open your head up so I can see how your brain works."

"What?"

Collin reached around to his back and withdrew a large hunting knife. Harper had no idea if it was hidden in his pants or in a sheath, but now she was officially terrified.

"I want to see how your brain works," Collin said. "Do you think your brain looks different compared to a normal person's because you can see and talk to ghosts?"

"I've never really considered it," Harper said.

"I'll compare it to your friend Zander's brain. Although, his might look different because he's a fairy. Do you think his brain looks different because he's a fairy?"

Harper felt sick to her stomach. Collin was gesturing wildly with the knife. Zander was somewhere unconscious in the kitchen. Molly was probably dead. Annie was as white as a ... well, ghost ... and utterly silent to her right. No one was coming to help. Harper was on her own and she had no idea what to do.

"I think you're sick," Harper said, fighting off tears. "I think that years of competing with your brother have made you sick. I think he's sick, too. I think you two feed off each other. You try to one-up one another. This is just your latest way of doing it."

"I love being psychoanalyzed," Collin said, a wide grin splitting his face. "My parents have sent me to therapy since I was thirteen and they found out I killed the neighbor's dog because it wouldn't stop yapping."

Collin threw himself on the couch and leaned back, resting his head on the pillow as he fingered the edge of the knife blade and stared at Harper, practically daring her to make a run for it.

"Keep on psychoanalyzing me," he said. "It's the only thing keeping you alive right now. You might as well have some fun before you die and tell me what you really think."

Harper decided to take him up on his suggestion. "You've got it."

JARED MOVED around Harper's house slowly, the hair on the back of his neck standing on end. There was a Jeep Cherokee in the driveway he didn't recognize and something felt "off" about the situation. He had no idea why he was on edge, but something told him to approach the house carefully.

He quietly stepped up on the patio, glad the outside light wasn't on so he could move closer to the window without detection. Someone would have to be staring directly at him to see him. He stared into the house.

He caught sight of Harper first, relief washing over him. *She was fine. He was overreacting. Nothing was wrong.* He told himself that over and over – and yet he didn't believe it.

Harper's face was white and she was standing ramrod straight in the middle of the living room. She was focused on the couch and whomever she was talking to was out of Jared's line of sight. He slipped farther down the outside wall of the house until he got to the window that looked into the kitchen. That room was lit up and Jared could see a prone body on the floor.

"Zander," he breathed, reaching for the gun on his belt.

Someone was in Harper's house and that someone had either incapacitated or killed Zander to get to Harper. Jared could only hope it was the former because if it was the latter he had a feeling Harper would never recover.

Jared moved to the back of the house, pulling his cell phone out of his pocket and texting Mel to bring backup before switching the phone to silent and shoving it back in his pocket. The smart thing to do was wait for backup. Jared's head told him that. His heart told him he needed to get to Harper now, though. It was his heart he listened to as he walked through the open kitchen door.

"I THINK your parents knew you were sick even before you killed the dog," Harper said. "I think your brother was always the favored child because they knew there was something wrong with you.

"I think you were smarter than Jay, but it didn't matter because he was better looking and your parents knew that he was going to amount to more than you were," she continued.

"That's fascinating," Collin said. "You might be right. Go on."

"I think the more Jay got his way in this world the more bitter you got," Harper said. "You wanted to be the special twin, but you couldn't be. Jay was always going to be ahead of you. Every time you found something you wanted, Jay took it away from you.

"You thought he was doing it as part of a competition," she said. "In a way he was. He knew there was something wrong with you, too, though. I think he was playing the same game you were – only he was out to win."

"I won," Collin countered. "I won because I'm the one who killed Annie and got away with it. I'm going to win again when I kill you and your little fairy boyfriend and get away with that. I thought of everything ... except the fact that you can talk to ghosts and that would come back to bite me. Once you're dead there's nothing to connect me to Annie. That's another win for me."

"What about Molly?" Harper asked.

"What about her?"

"People know you were out on a date with her tonight," Harper said.

"*You* know I was out on a date with her," Collin countered. "Jay does, too, but he would never suspect me of doing something heinous like killing Miss Molly. I'll tell everyone she changed her mind and took off on her own."

"Jared knows, too," Harper said, relishing having the upper hand on at least one thing.

Collin stilled. "What? The cop? How?"

"He was at the coffee shop with me when Molly told me about the date," Harper replied. "You'll be his prime suspect."

"No, that's not possible," Collin said. "Molly never mentioned seeing him this afternoon."

"That doesn't change the fact that it's the truth," Harper said. "Our other co-worker knows, too. Zander told him this afternoon." It was a lie, but Harper was hoping it would be enough to scare Collin out of his course of action. There was no way he could get to Jared and Eric and kill them, too. He had to realize that.

"Well, this sucks," Collin complained. "Now I'm going to have to kill a cop. Do you know what a pain that's going to be?"

"Probably more than you realize," Jared said, stepping into the room with his gun drawn.

Harper had never been more relieved to see anyone in her entire life and she wanted to run to him. Unfortunately, Collin was already on his feet and reaching for her before she had a chance to react.

Collin grabbed Harper's arm and dragged her in front of him, lifting the knife to her throat in a menacing manner as he eyed Jared. "Sonovabitch!"

"I had a feeling it was you," Jared said, fighting to keep himself calm despite the deadly weapon pressing into Harper's throat. He sent her a reassuring look before focusing all of his attention on Collin. "Don't you want to know how?"

"Not particularly," Collin said, glancing around the room as he searched for an escape route. "Stay over there. If you move any closer I'll kill her."

"If you hurt her I will rip your throat out and show it to you before you die," Jared promised.

"Did you see Zander?" Harper asked, a lone tear slipping down her cheek. "Is he okay?"

"He's unconscious in the kitchen," Jared answered. "He'll be fine."

"Not once I'm done with him," Collin said.

"You're not getting near him," Jared countered. "He's in the kitchen behind me. You don't have a card to play. I texted for backup before I came into this house. My partner just happens to be Zander's uncle. He'll be here any minute – and he won't be alone."

"Well, isn't that just a kick in the pants," Collin mused. "What you're basically telling me is that I'm screwed no matter what."

"I guess so," Jared said, his hands steady on the gun as he kept it pointed in Collin's direction. "The only choice you have is how hard you go down."

"Oh, I have one more choice," Collin said. "If I do what you say I'm going to prison. I don't think I'd do well in prison. If I do what I want, I'll get to watch Harper die and then you'll kill me. I think that's going to be my best option. I won't suffer that way."

"You're not doing a thing to her!"

"Oh, Copper, listen to you," Collin taunted. "You're infatuated with her, aren't you? Do you love her? Do you think you're going to fall in love with her? Do you have visions of hot sex and cuddling together over cold winter nights running through your head?"

Jared didn't answer.

"What if I take that from you?" Collin asked, pressing the blade of the knife into Harper's exposed neck and causing her to whimper.

"I will kill you," Jared seethed.

"If I kill her will you cry?" Collin asked. "Will you mourn her for a few months or a few years? Will you ever get over losing her? I get the feeling that you two are just starting. You have hope. I see it on both of your faces.

"I had hope, too," he continued. "I had hope that Annie would be my special someone. Instead she slept with my brother and crushed me. She even took photos of that so I could relive the experience over and over again."

"I don't care about any of that," Jared said matter-of-factly. "I don't care about your perceived reasons for being a psychopath. I don't care if your brother gave you a wedgie every day of your life. All I care about in this situation is Harper."

"That's why I want to kill her," Collin said. "The last thing I see is going to be your face as you watch her die."

"Either drop the knife or I'm going to drop you."

Collin tilted his head to the side, feigning like he was actually considering the offer. "No," he said, shaking his head. "I'm going to kill her instead."

He drew the knife back, making as if he was going to plunge it into Harper's throat. She cried out in terror as she tried to move away, managing to put a few inches between her and Collin before he could stab her.

Jared didn't hesitate. He pulled the trigger. The deafening roar of the gun wasn't enough to drown out Harper's screams, but Jared held steady and did his duty. He never blinked.

HARPER'S HEART was pounding so hard she was convinced she was having a heart attack. She instinctively reached for her chest, imagining a gunshot wound spreading red blood across her simple white T-shirt.

She didn't feel any pain. She figured she was in shock.

Then Collin's body dropped to the floor behind her and Harper realized Jared's aim was as true as his heart.

"Come here, sweetie," Jared said, motioning for Harper to close the gap between them as he kept his gun trained on Collin.

Harper rushed to him, burying her face in his chest as he held her. He ran his hands down her shaking back and kissed her cheek. "It's okay now. It's okay."

The front door of the house flew open and Mel raced inside, his own weapon drawn.

"He's down," Jared said, refusing to release Harper and instead drawing her closer.

"Where is Zander?" Mel asked.

"He's unconscious in the kitchen."

"I brought paramedics," Mel said, moving around the edge of the couch so he could study Collin. "You were right. It was Collin."

"That doesn't make me feel like I've won anything," Jared said.

"Is he dead?"

"I shot him in the head. It was the only clear shot I had."

"I'm not shedding any tears over it," Mel said. "I'm going to get the paramedics and check on Zander. You're sure he's alive, right?"

"I checked him when I came in," Jared replied, his hand never stilling as he rubbed soothing circles along Harper's back as she sobbed in his arms. "He was breathing fine. It looks like he's going to have a knot on his head. I think Collin surprised him. The only thing truly hurt in all this is probably going to be his ego because he missed out on all the excitement and getting to beat Collin up himself."

"I hope you're right," Mel said.

Harper pulled her tear-streaked face away from Jared and glanced at Mel. "Check Collin's vehicle," she said, her voice shaky. "I ... he said he killed Molly. I'm guessing he still had her body with him."

Jared wanted to kill Collin all over again. "We've got it," he said. He slipped his gun back into the holster, freeing both hands so he could pull Harper tight against his chest. "We've got it. You're okay."

"Am I?"

"You're going to be okay," Jared said, pressing his lips to her forehead. "I'm going to make sure of it."

TWENTY-SIX

Jared moved Harper out to the side patio so the tech team could go over the scene without interruptions. He settled her on one of the lounge chairs, sitting behind her and pulling her back against his chest as he proceeded to rock her.

"It's going to be okay," he murmured into her hair.

"I need to see Zander."

"The paramedics are working on him," Jared said, pointing to the driveway where he could clearly see Zander standing of his own volition. He looked like he was arguing with one of the paramedics. "He looks okay."

"I thought ... ."

"I know," Jared said. "He's okay."

"Molly is okay, too," Mel said, appearing at the edge of the patio.

Hope welled in Harper's chest. "She is? Collin said that he killed her."

"I think he was planning on getting to her after he got to you," Mel replied. "We had to take her to the hospital. It looks like she was drugged. They're going to flush her system there, but she was conscious."

"Did you talk to her?"

"She was loopy and out of it, but she was forming words."

"I need to go to the hospital to make sure she's okay," Harper said, moving to get off the lounge chair.

"I'll take you in a few minutes," Jared said, tugging her back down and wrapping his arms around her. He needed to hold her. He barely knew her and yet the idea of letting her go right now filled him with dread.

"I'm going to need your weapon, too," Mel said. "You have to be cleared in the shooting."

"I figured," Jared said, leaning forward to give Mel access to his holstered gun. "Go ahead and take it."

Mel grabbed the gun and slipped it into a bag, smiling kindly at Harper as he looked her over. "You look rough, kid."

"I feel rough," Harper admitted. "I thought Collin killed Zander. I didn't know what to do. I kind of ... froze."

"You're alive," Mel said. "That's all that matters. You're all alive."

"Not all of us," Harper murmured, her gaze falling on Annie.

"I'm going to leave you two alone for a few minutes," Mel said. "Before you take Harper to the hospital I need a statement from you, Jared."

Jared nodded mutely. Once Mel was gone Annie spoke. "I'm sorry this happened to you because of me," Annie said. "I didn't remember until I saw him putting Molly in the back of his truck."

"It's over with now," Harper said. "It's all ... done."

"I just wanted to be loved," Annie said. "I didn't know it would be hate that ended me."

"You can go now," Harper said softly, leaning back into Jared who merely watched her talk to empty air. "There's no reason to stay now. Collin is gone."

"He won't be ... there ... will he?"

"No. He'll go to another place."

"Have you seen that place, too?" Annie asked.

"Only once. You'll go to the good place. Don't worry."

"How do I go?" Annie asked.

"Pick a star and make a wish," Harper said. "All you have to want to do is crossover and it will happen."

"Thank you for everything," Annie said.

"Have a good ... forever," Harper said, sighing as Annie began to dissolve in front of her eyes. "Goodbye."

Jared waited a few minutes before he spoke again. "Is she gone?"

"She's gone."

"Are you okay?"

"I'm ... tired. I feel like I've been run over by a truck and then backed over again."

Jared chuckled, his own weariness overtaking him. "I can see that. Are you ready for me to take you to the hospital?"

"Yeah. I need to check on Zander first."

"I'll give my statement to Mel while you're doing that," Jared said. "I'm sure Zander will want to go with us ... that is if they don't make him take his own ride to the hospital."

"I didn't thank you," Harper said, realization dawning. "You saved me."

"I think I saved us both," Jared said. "You don't have to thank me, though."

"How come you came to the house?"

"I wanted to see you. I thought we could have a beer and talk. I don't know what made me come here."

"I think it was destiny."

"Maybe," Jared conceded. He pushed Harper forward and physically turned her body to the side so he could study her. "You look tired." He ran his thumb down her cheek.

"I feel tired ... but okay. You saved my life. Zander and Molly are alive. Annie moved on. Things could've been a whole lot worse."

"I really want to kiss you right now," Jared admitted. "I'm not sure if it's the right time, though."

Harper didn't bother to answer him. Instead she pressed her lips to his, waiting for the surprise to vacate his body before he pulled her close and sank into the kiss. It wasn't a hot and sexy kiss. It wasn't full of need or desire. It was a culmination of everything they both wanted, though, and it was a promise of things to come.

When they finally parted, Harper's eyes were wide as she ran her fingers over her lips. "That was ... nice."

"It was," Jared agreed. "The next one will be even better."

"When will that be?"

Jared grinned. "Right now."

This time when he pulled her to him the kiss was an expression of need, want, and desire – and a continuing promise of things to come.

It was only the beginning, but both of them were looking forward to the adventure.

Want more? Sign up for my mailing list. It's for new releases only, no spam.

http://eepurl.com/bLFbgz

Made in the USA
Middletown, DE
10 March 2025